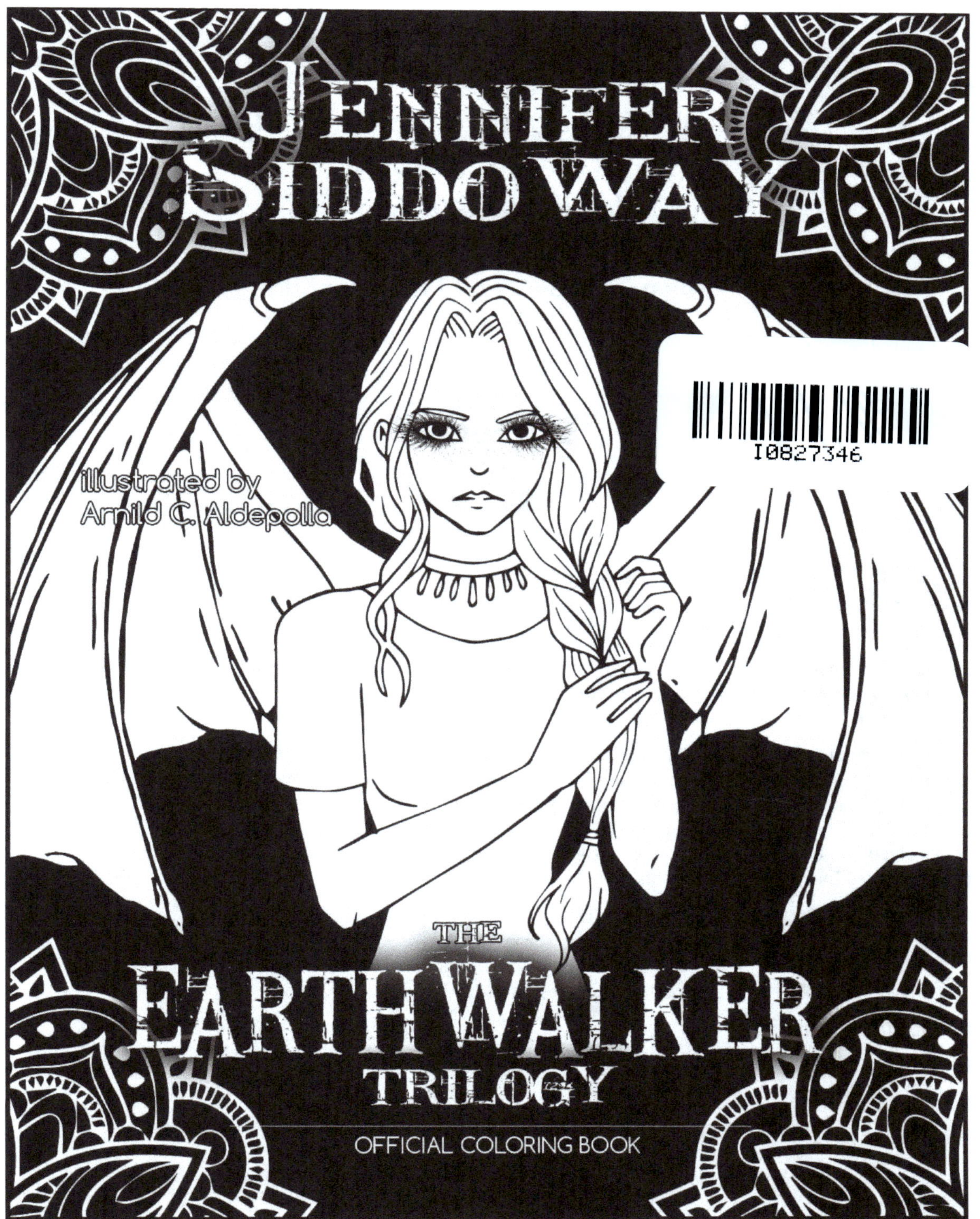
Jennifer
Siddoway
illustrated by
Arnild C. Aldepolla
The
EarthWalker
Trilogy
Official Coloring Book

The Earthwalker Trilogy was written by:

Jennifer Siddoway

Illustrated by: Arnild C. Aldepolla

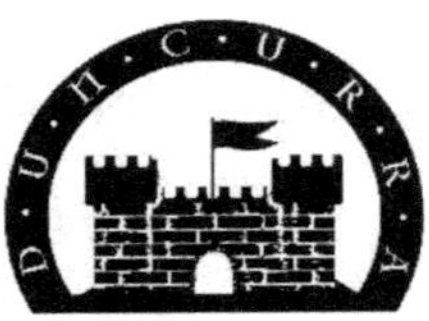

Dealing with the Devil (The Earthwalker Trilogy Book 1) - Second Edition

www.duncurra.com

ISBN: 978-1-942623-98-4

Produced in the USA

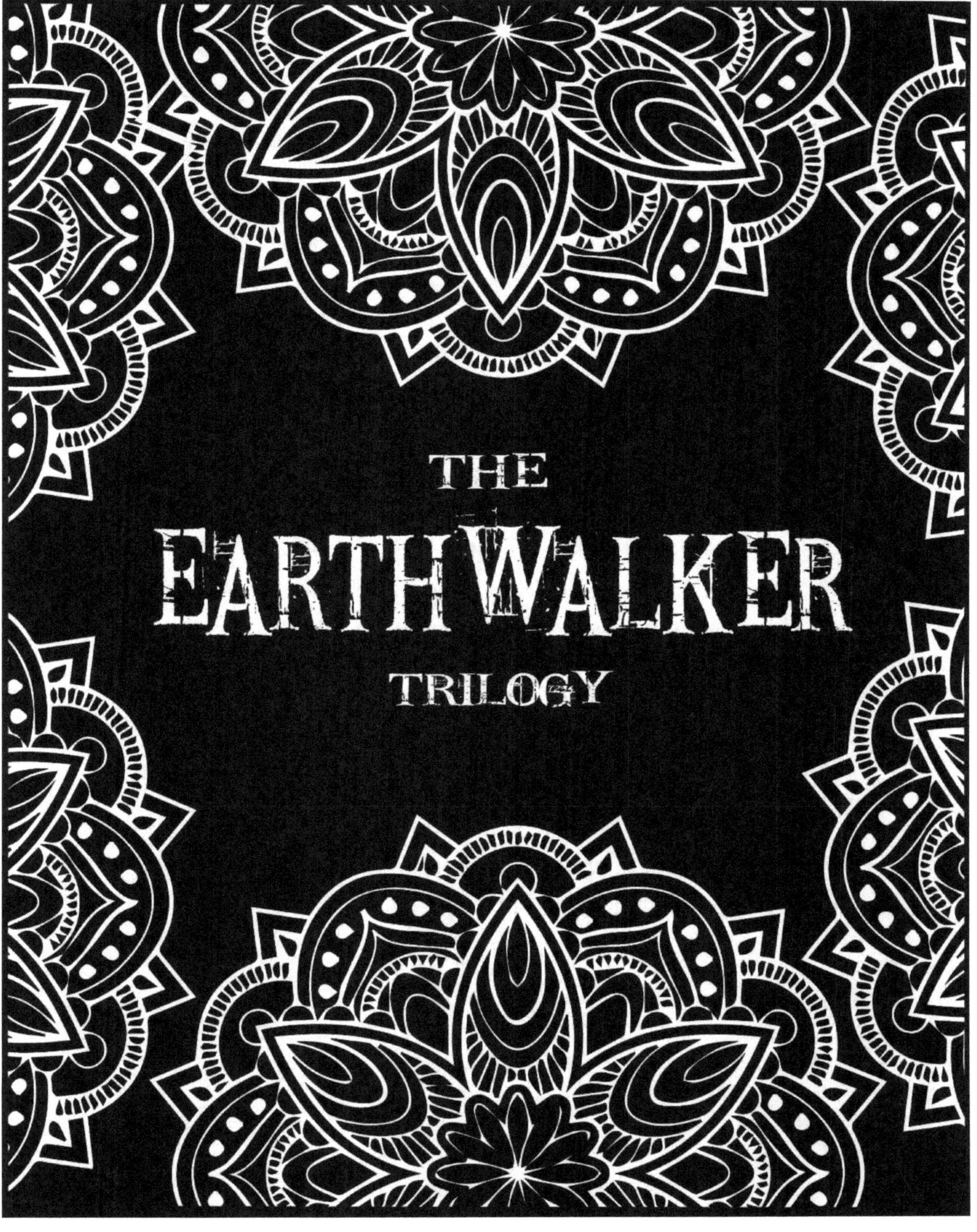
THE
EARTHWALKER
TRILOGY

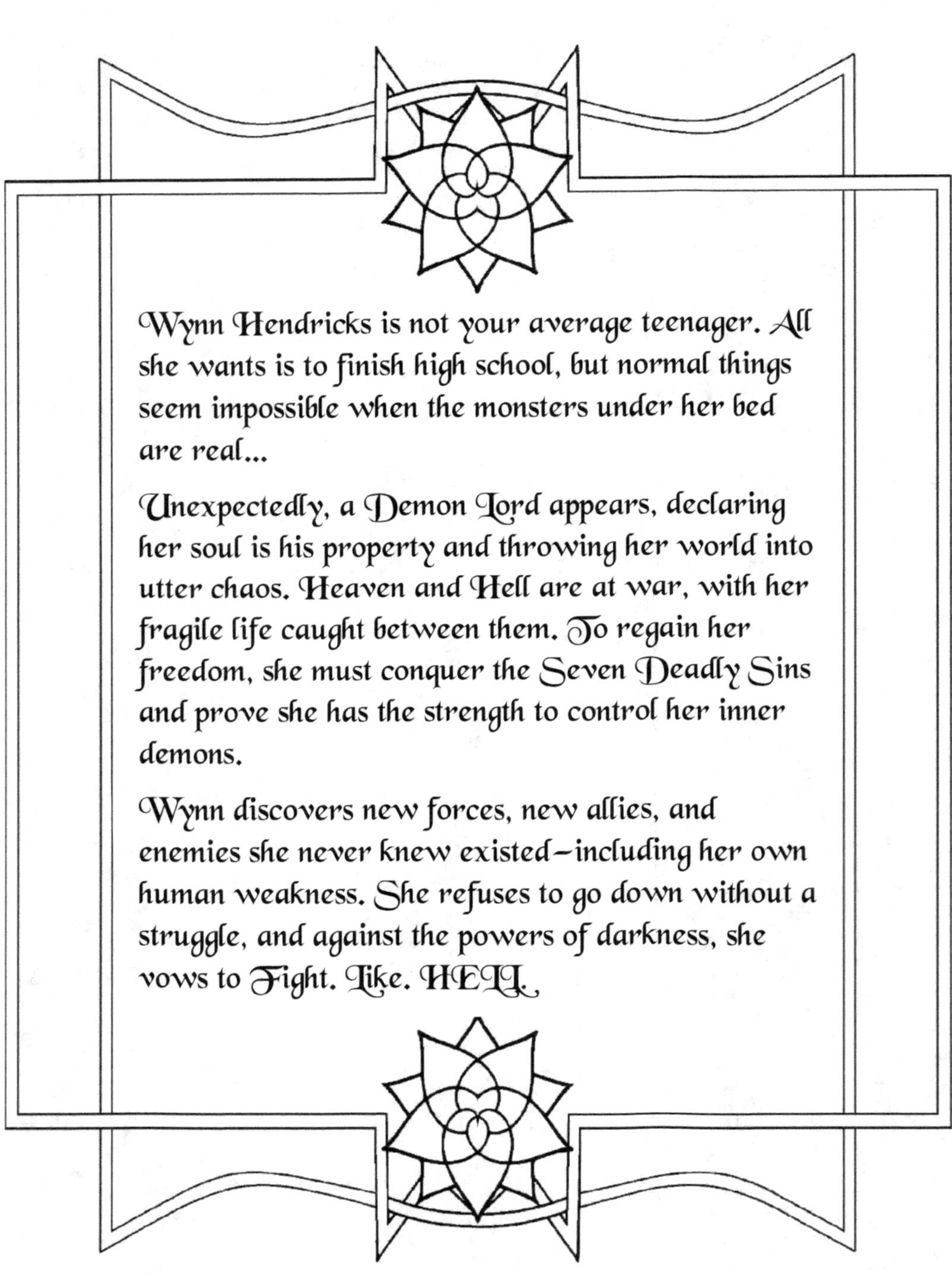

Wynn Hendricks is not your average teenager. All she wants is to finish high school, but normal things seem impossible when the monsters under her bed are real...

Unexpectedly, a Demon Lord appears, declaring her soul is his property and throwing her world into utter chaos. Heaven and Hell are at war, with her fragile life caught between them. To regain her freedom, she must conquer the Seven Deadly Sins and prove she has the strength to control her inner demons.

Wynn discovers new forces, new allies, and enemies she never knew existed—including her own human weakness. She refuses to go down without a struggle, and against the powers of darkness, she vows to Fight. Like. HELL.

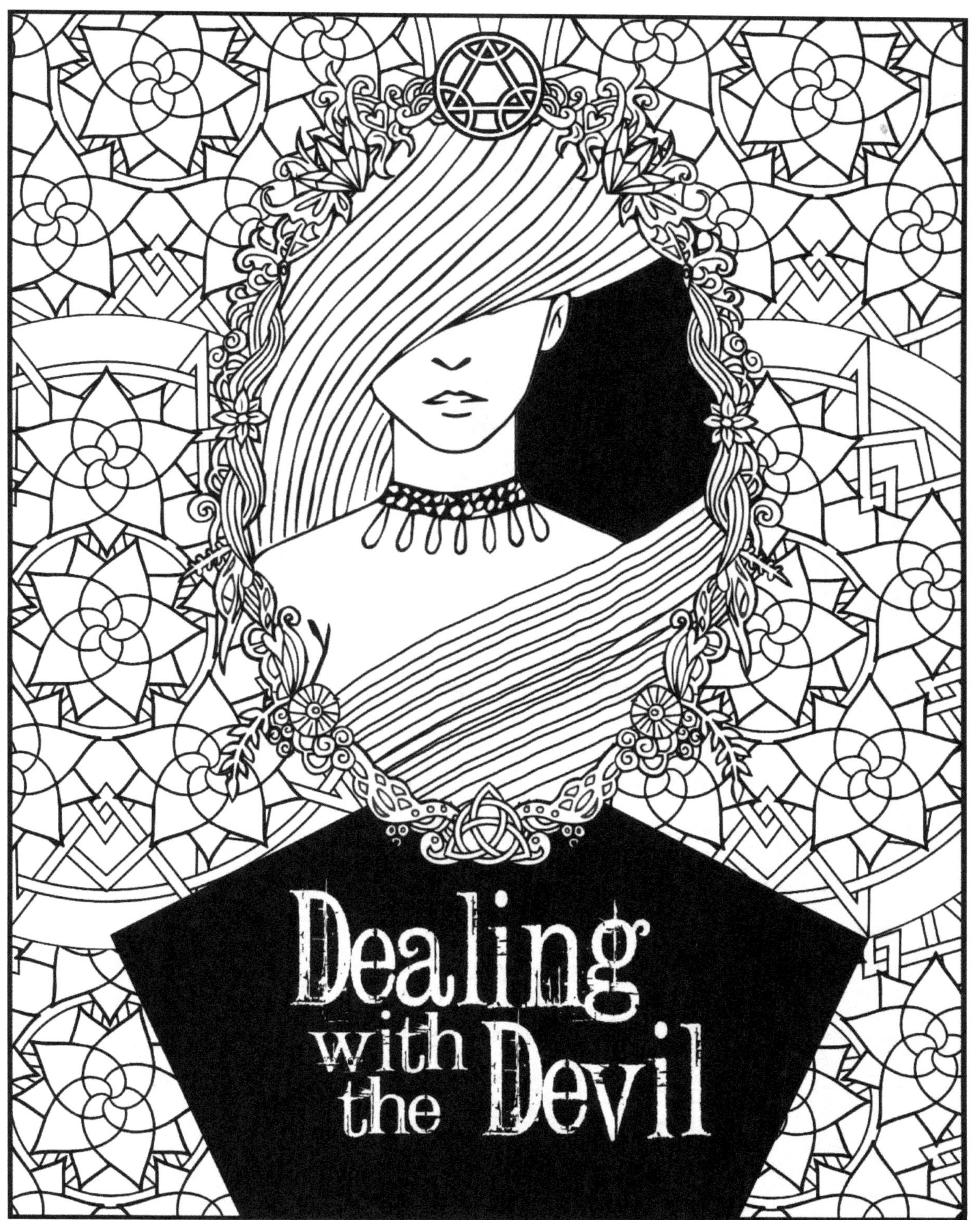
Dealing
with the Devil

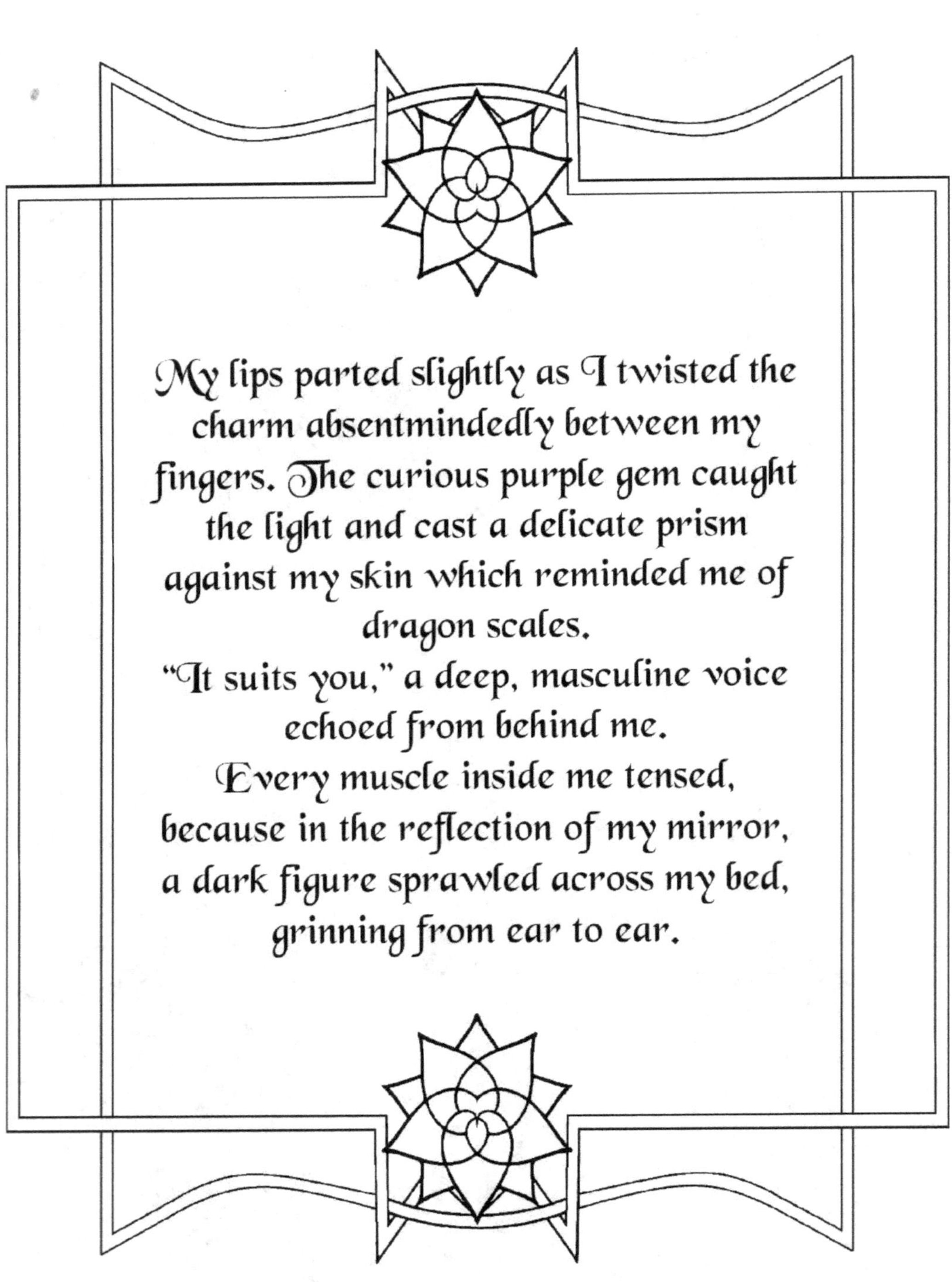

My lips parted slightly as I twisted the charm absentmindedly between my fingers. The curious purple gem caught the light and cast a delicate prism against my skin which reminded me of dragon scales.

"It suits you," a deep, masculine voice echoed from behind me.

Every muscle inside me tensed, because in the reflection of my mirror, a dark figure sprawled across my bed, grinning from ear to ear.

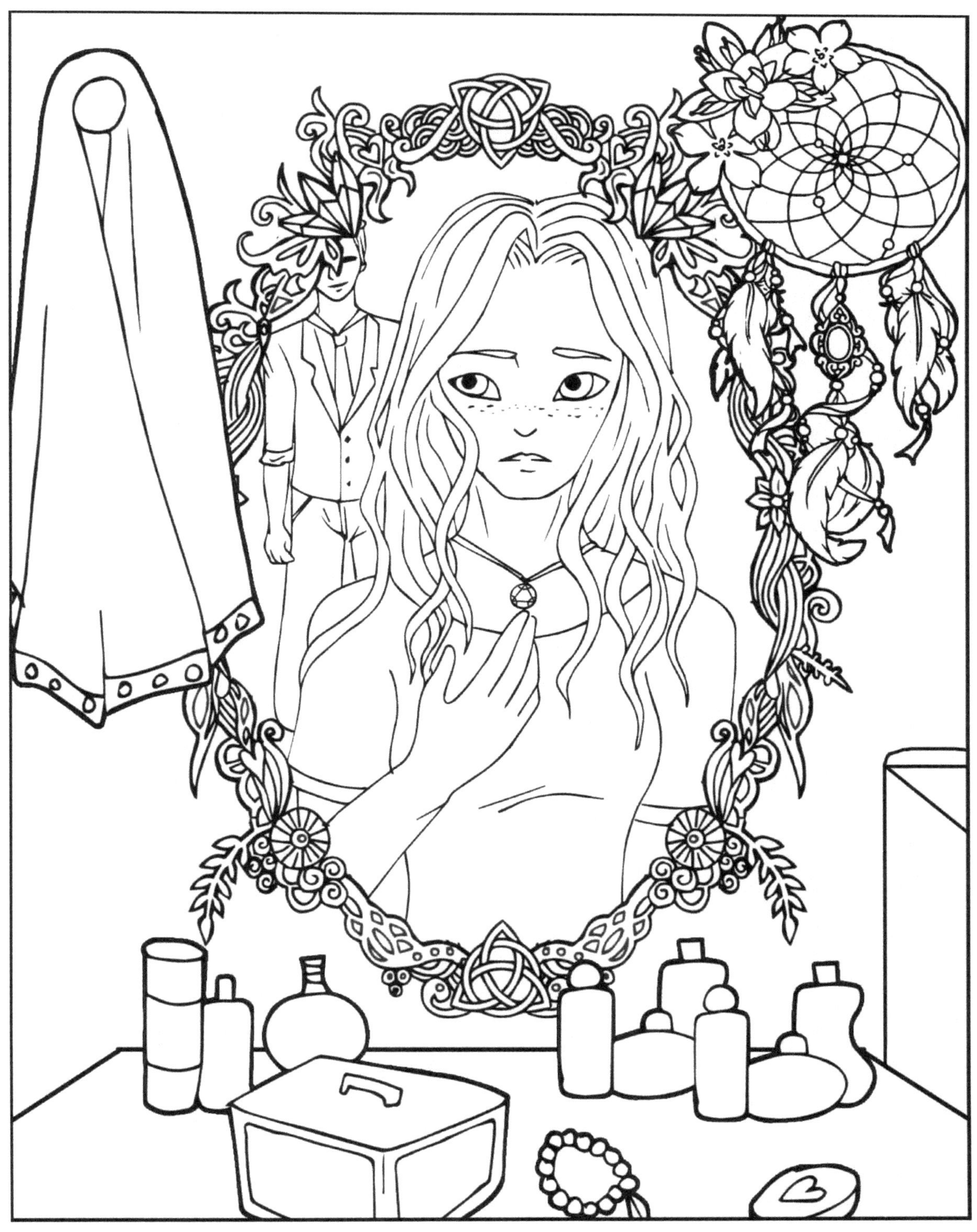

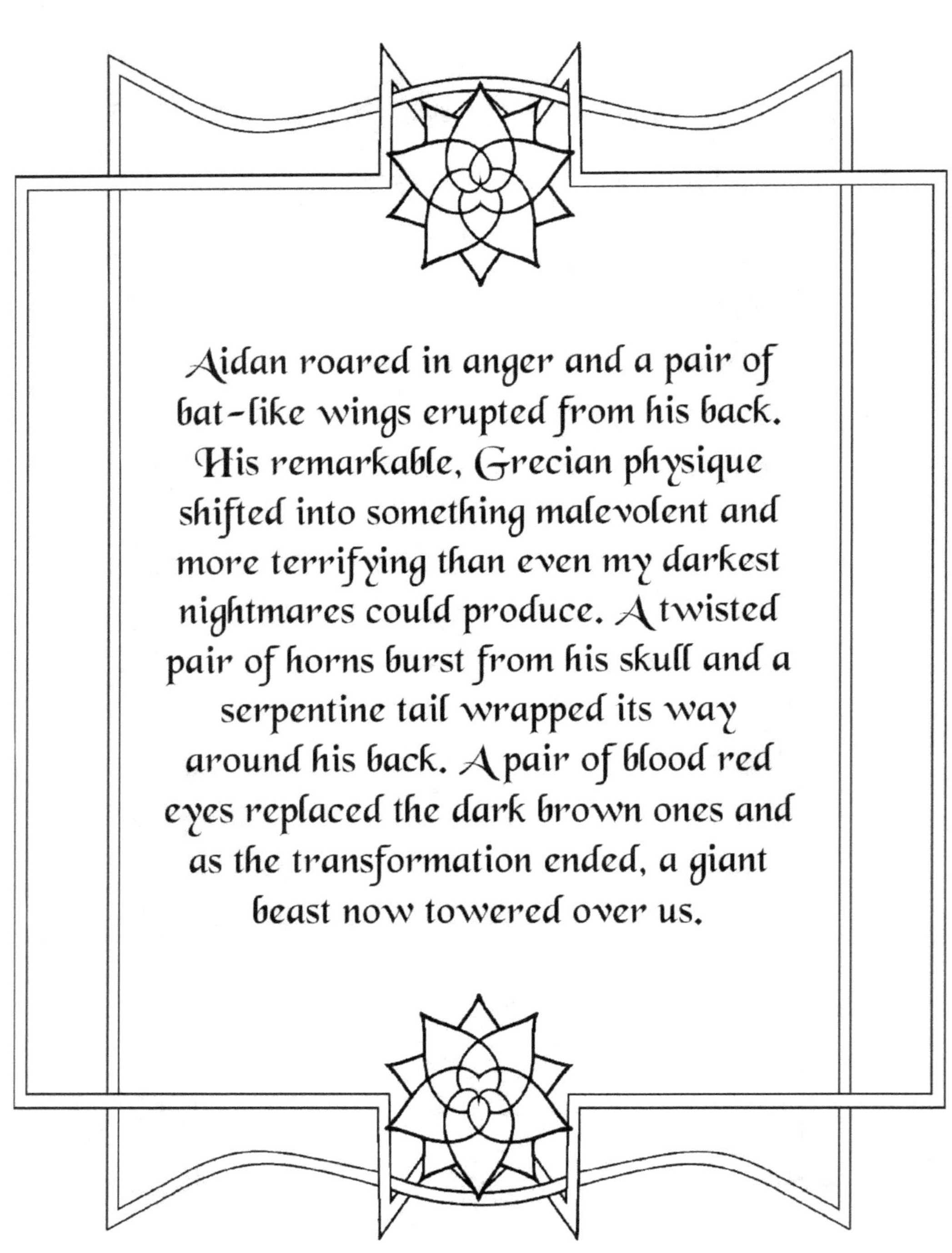

Aidan roared in anger and a pair of bat-like wings erupted from his back. His remarkable, Grecian physique shifted into something malevolent and more terrifying than even my darkest nightmares could produce. A twisted pair of horns burst from his skull and a serpentine tail wrapped its way around his back. A pair of blood red eyes replaced the dark brown ones and as the transformation ended, a giant beast now towered over us.

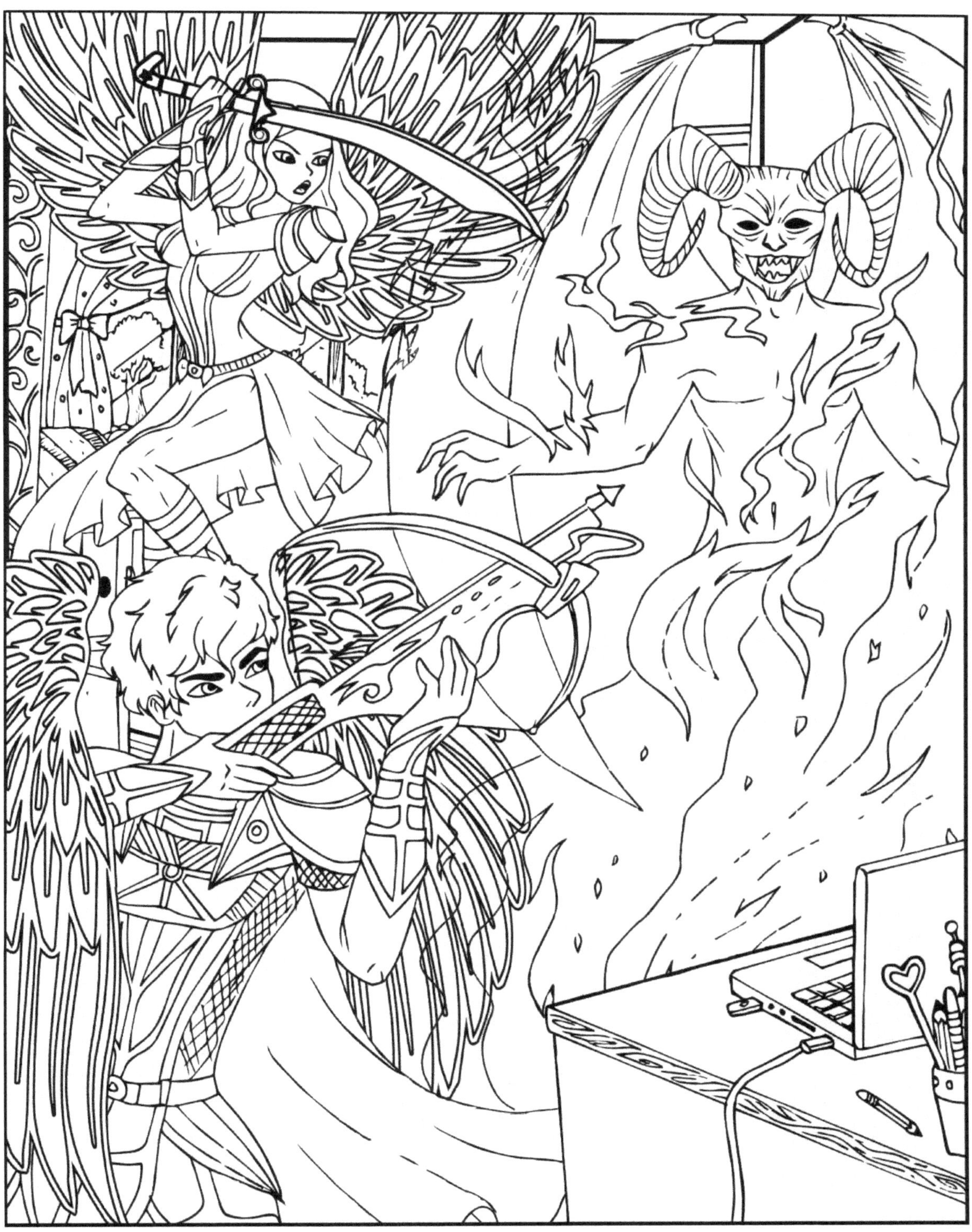

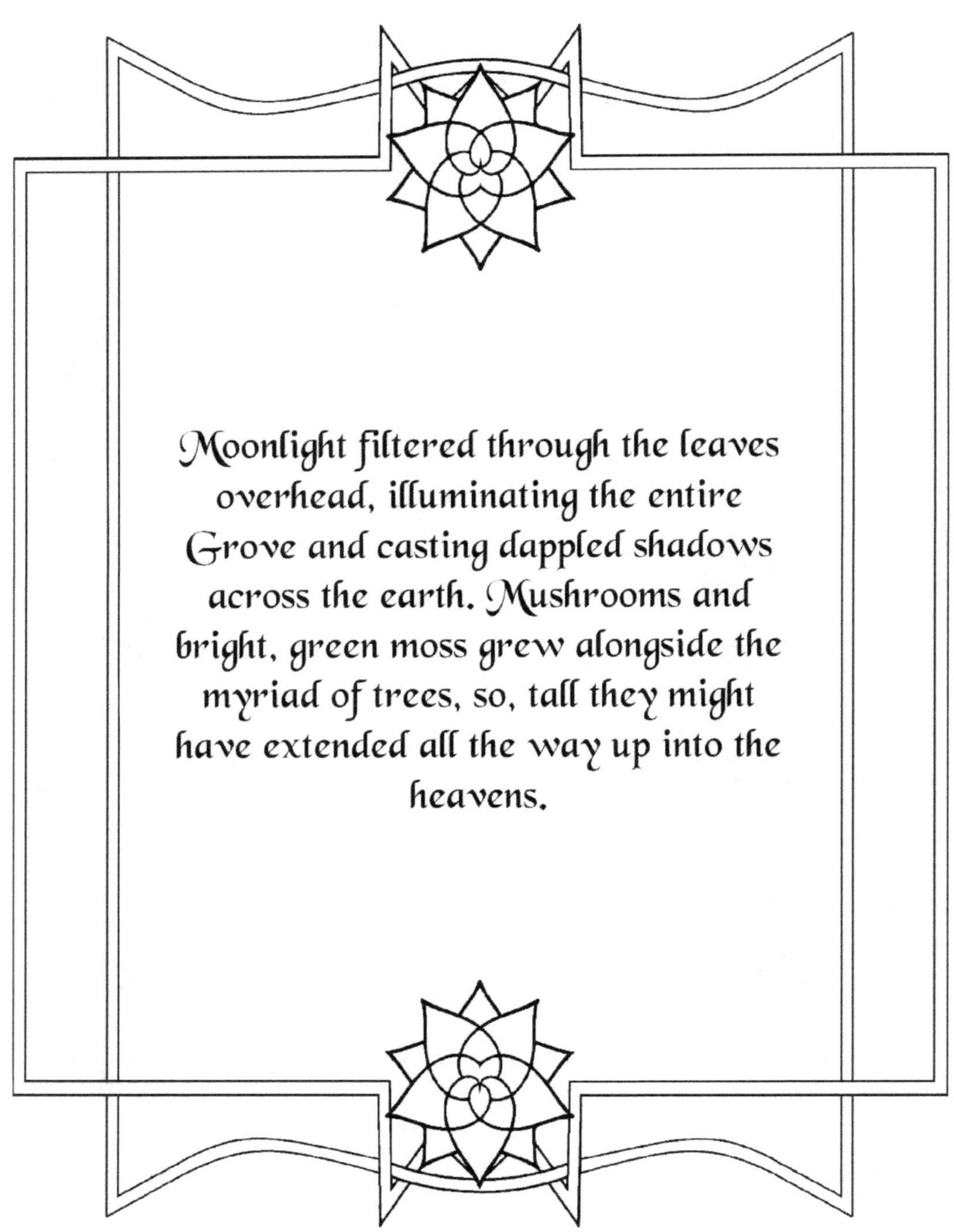

Moonlight filtered through the leaves overhead, illuminating the entire Grove and casting dappled shadows across the earth. Mushrooms and bright, green moss grew alongside the myriad of trees, so, tall they might have extended all the way up into the heavens.

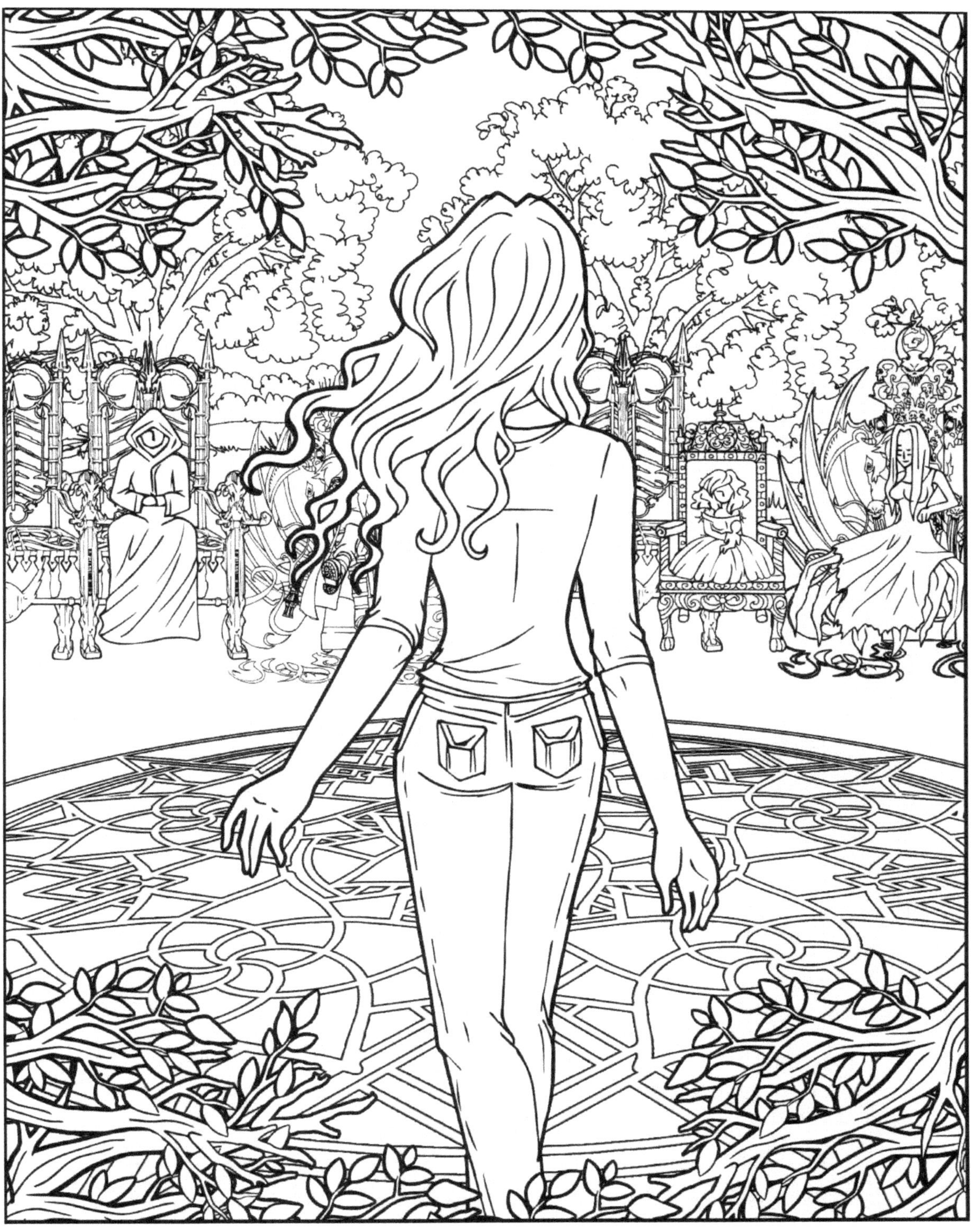

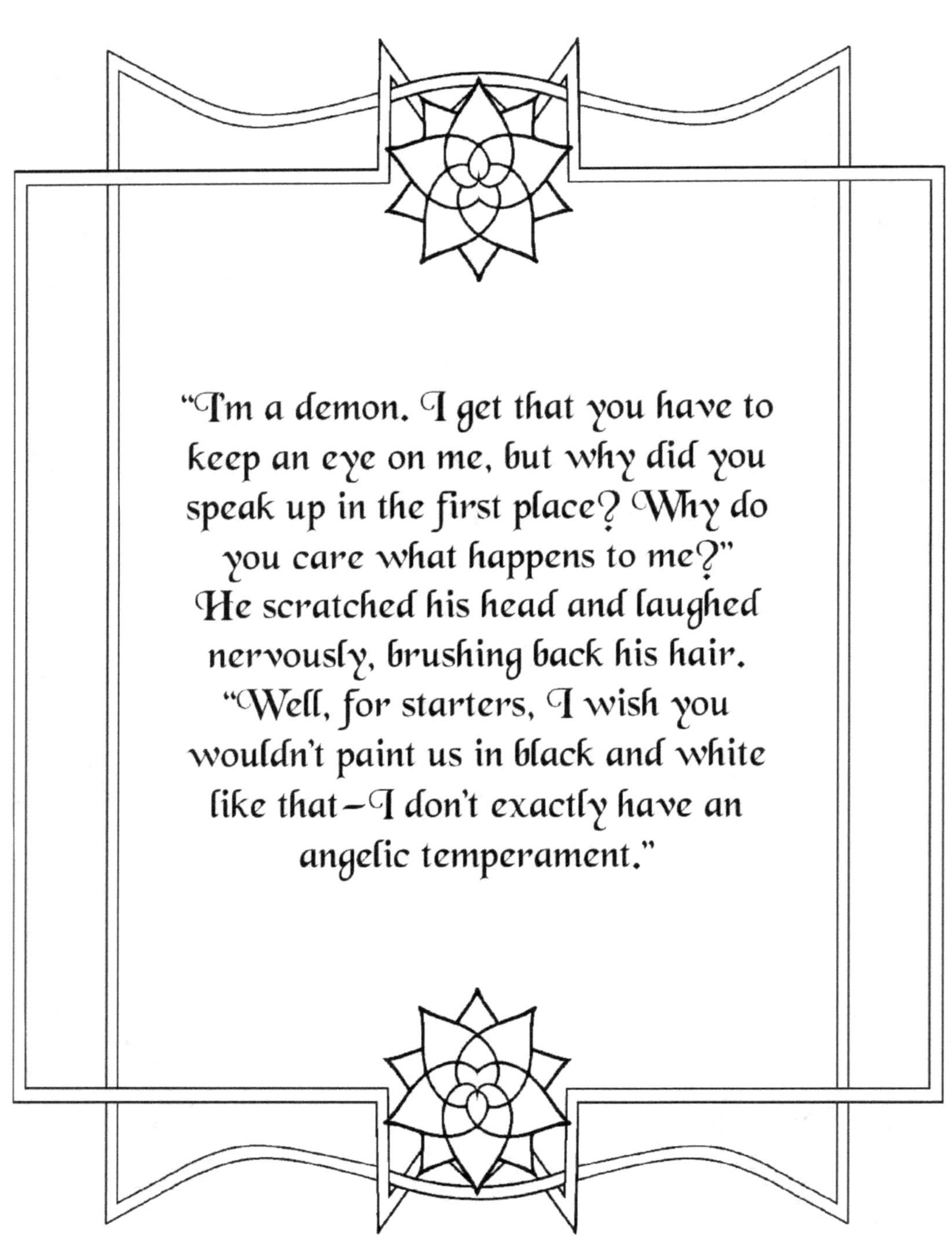

"I'm a demon. I get that you have to keep an eye on me, but why did you speak up in the first place? Why do you care what happens to me?"

He scratched his head and laughed nervously, brushing back his hair.

"Well, for starters, I wish you wouldn't paint us in black and white like that—I don't exactly have an angelic temperament."

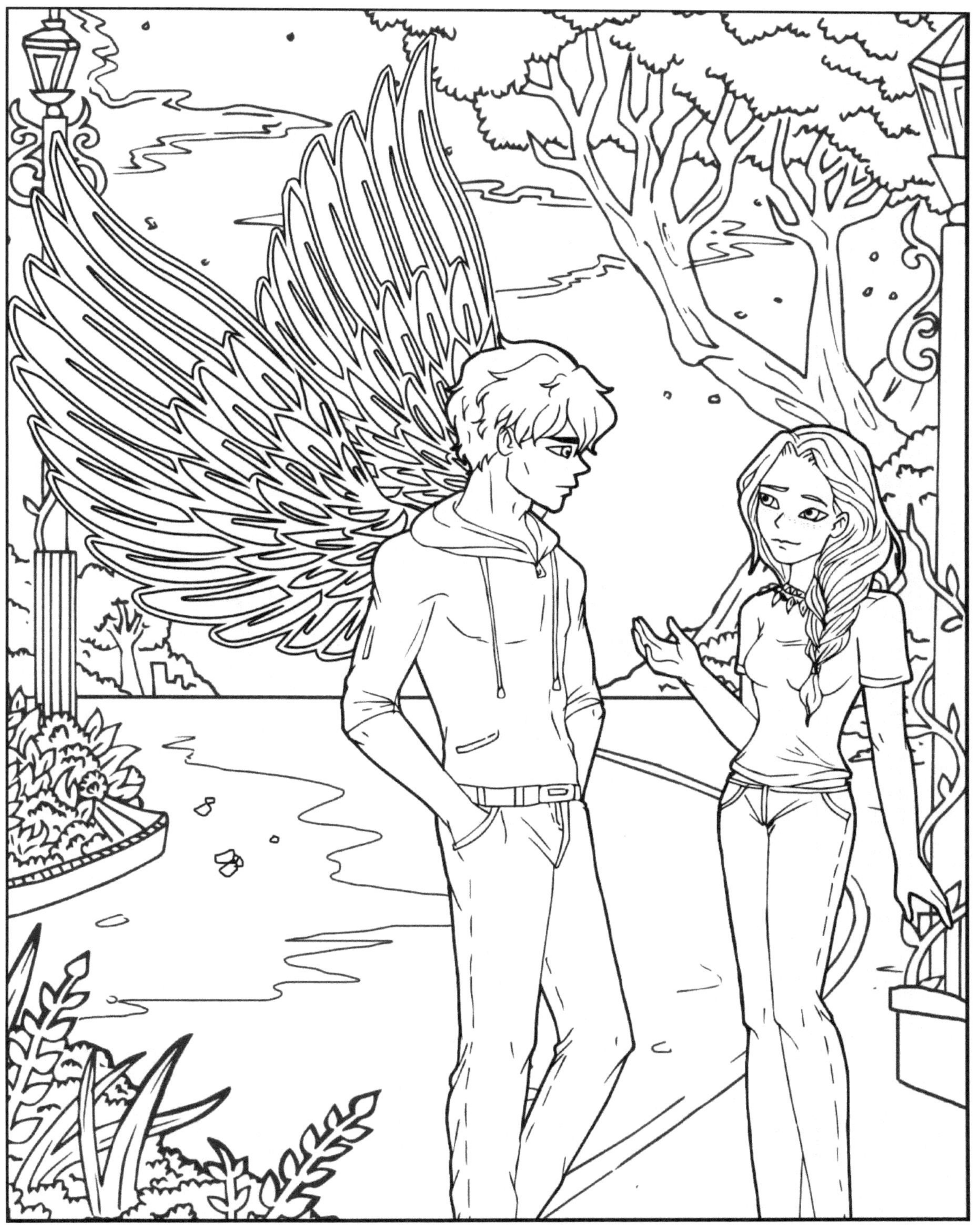

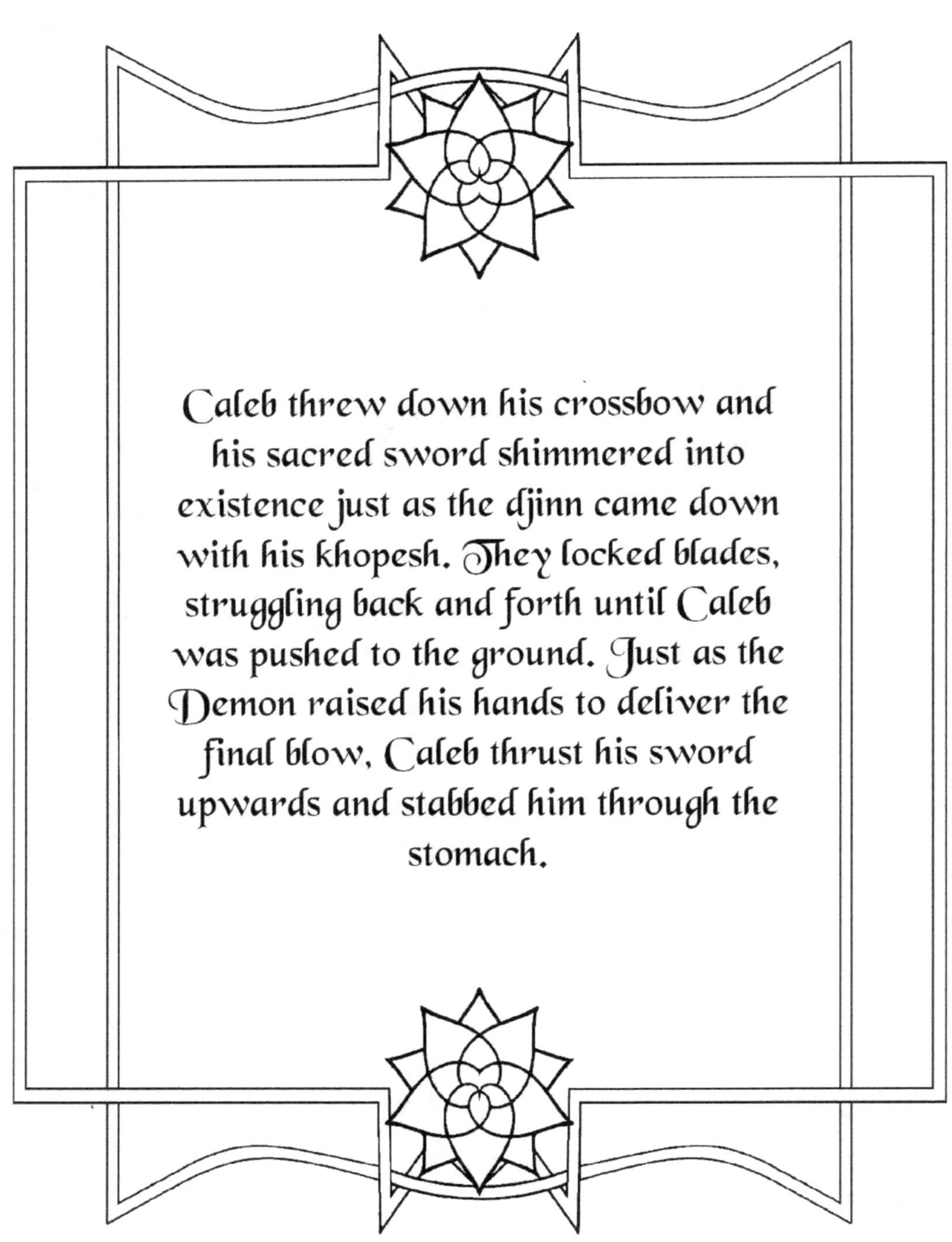

Caleb threw down his crossbow and his sacred sword shimmered into existence just as the djinn came down with his khopesh. They locked blades, struggling back and forth until Caleb was pushed to the ground. Just as the Demon raised his hands to deliver the final blow, Caleb thrust his sword upwards and stabbed him through the stomach.

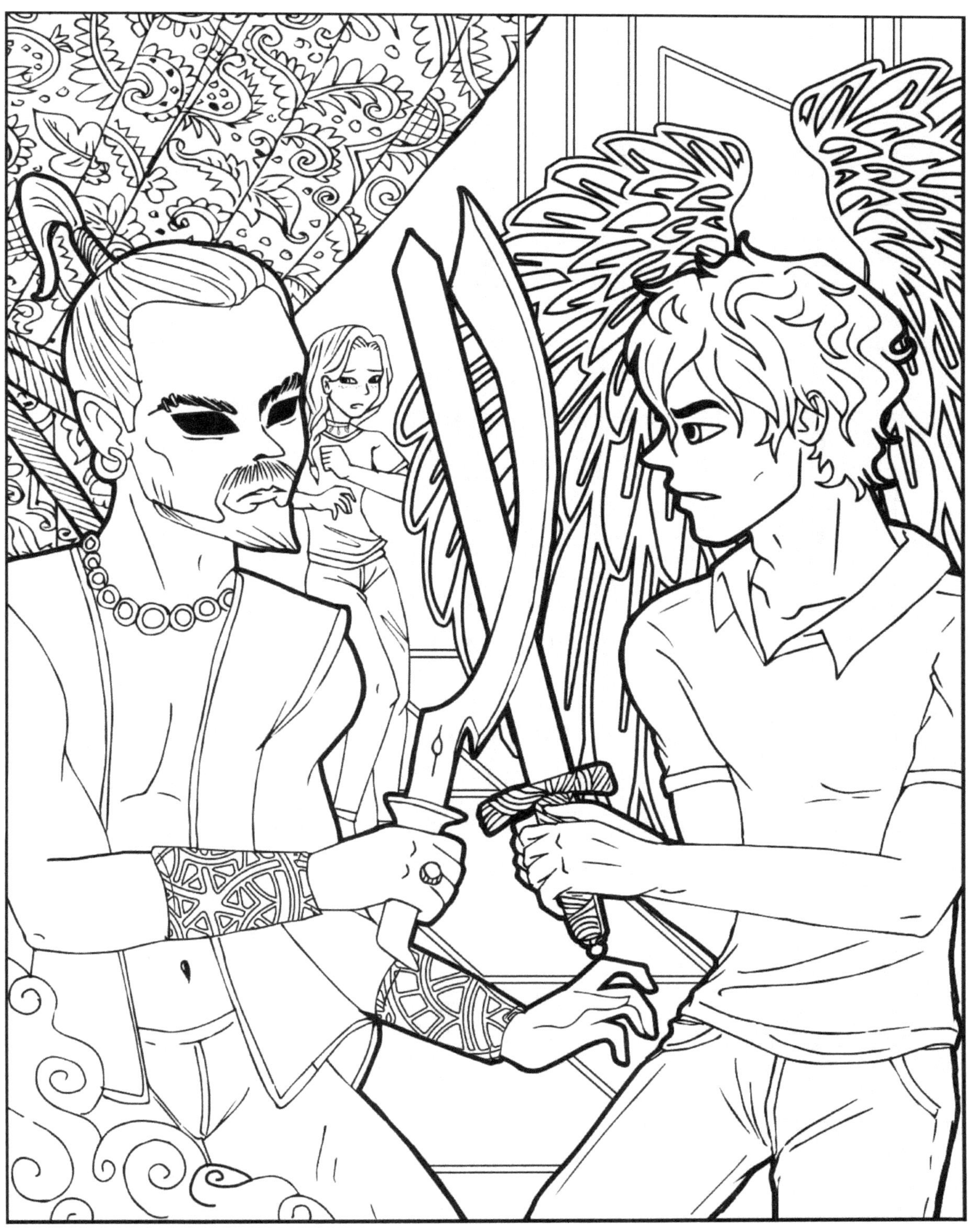

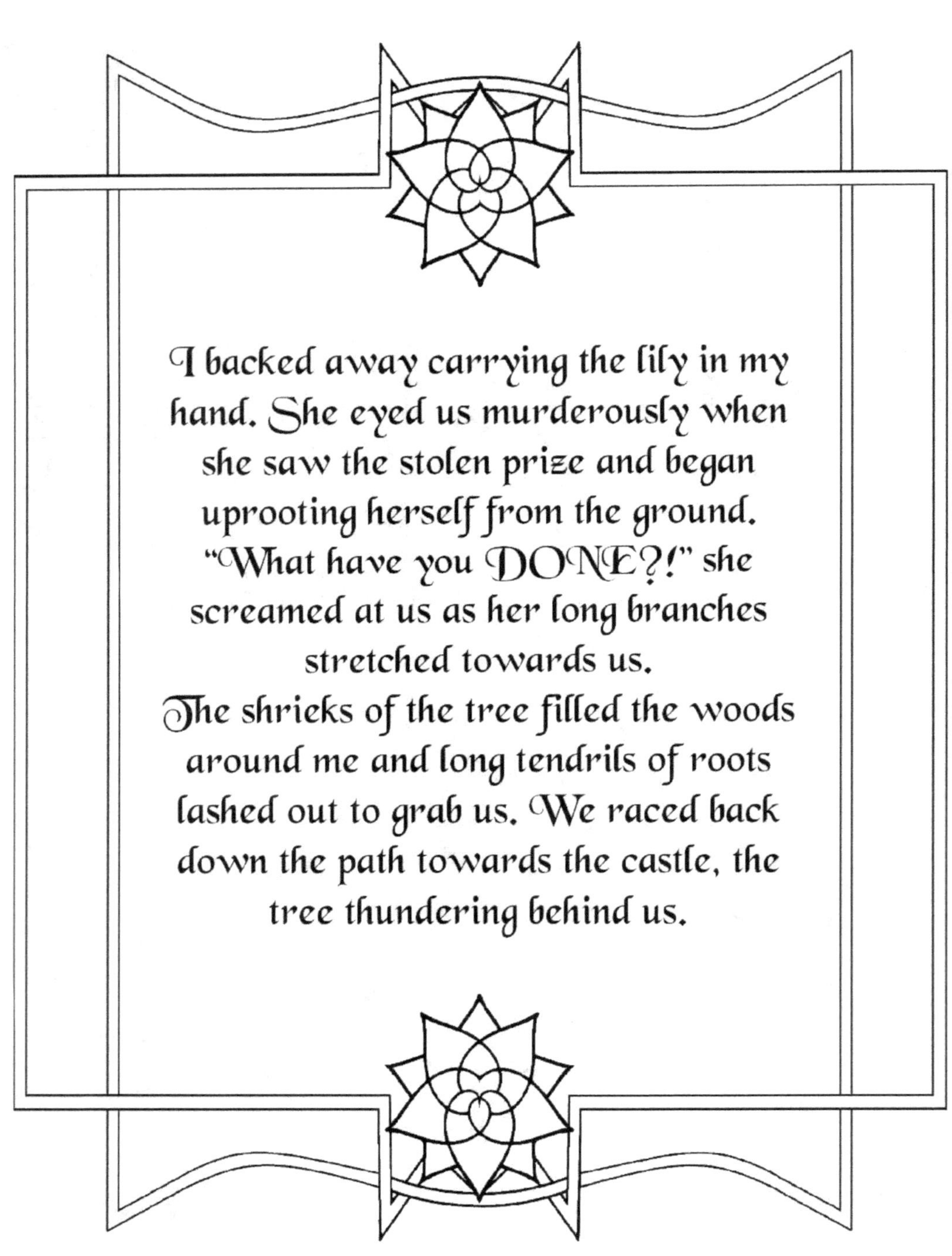

I backed away carrying the lily in my hand. She eyed us murderously when she saw the stolen prize and began uprooting herself from the ground. "What have you DONE?!" she screamed at us as her long branches stretched towards us.
The shrieks of the tree filled the woods around me and long tendrils of roots lashed out to grab us. We raced back down the path towards the castle, the tree thundering behind us.

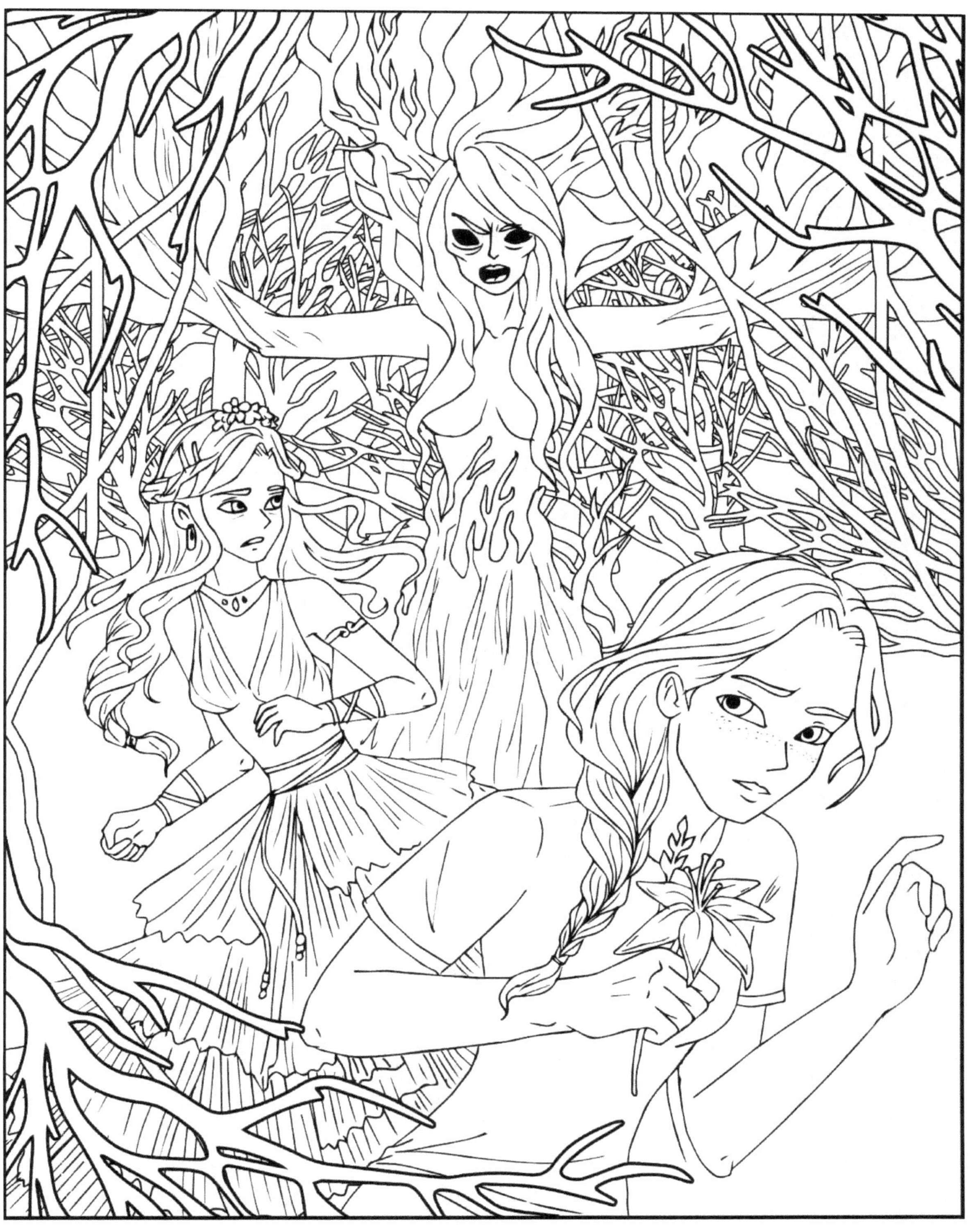

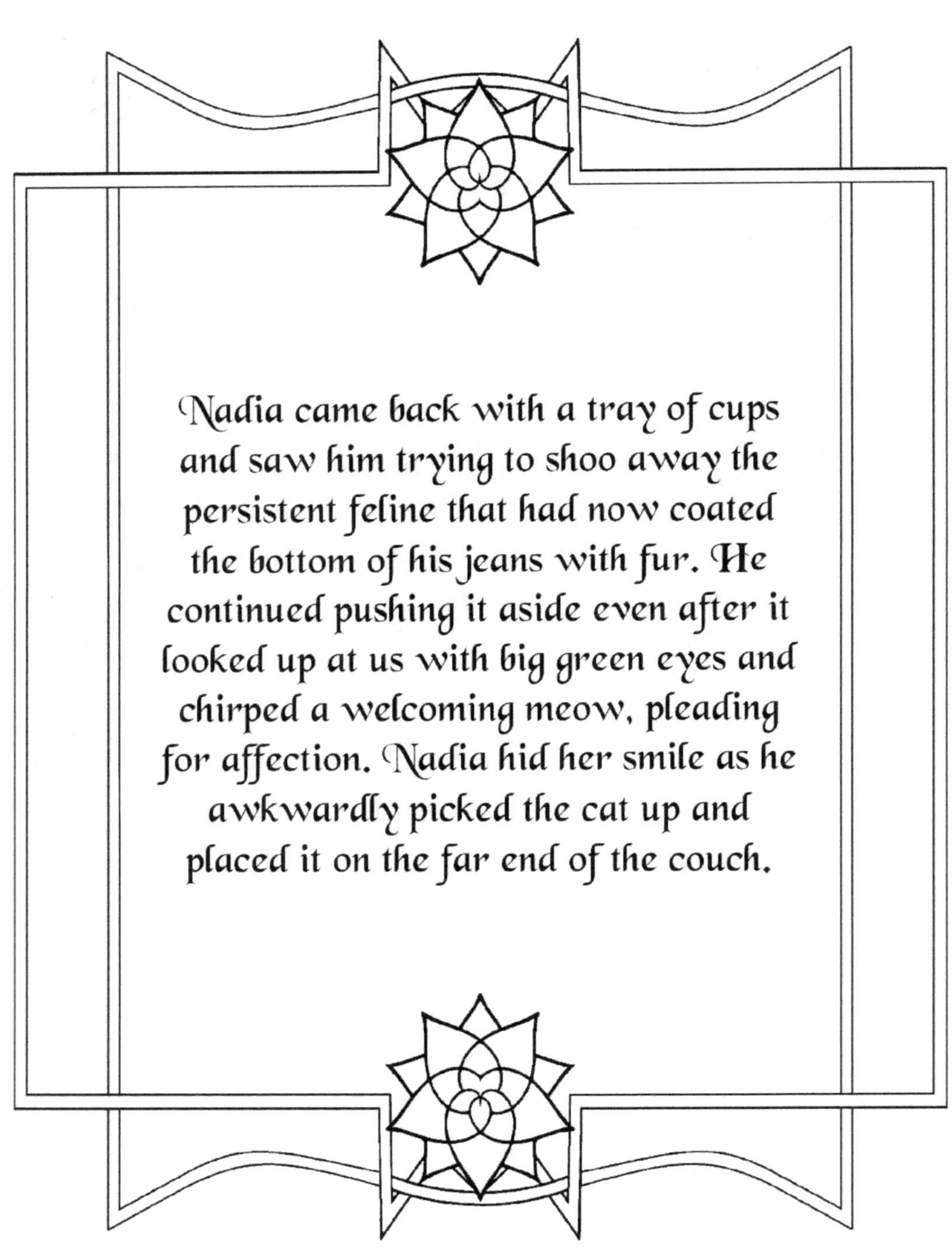

Nadia came back with a tray of cups and saw him trying to shoo away the persistent feline that had now coated the bottom of his jeans with fur. He continued pushing it aside even after it looked up at us with big green eyes and chirped a welcoming meow, pleading for affection. Nadia hid her smile as he awkwardly picked the cat up and placed it on the far end of the couch.

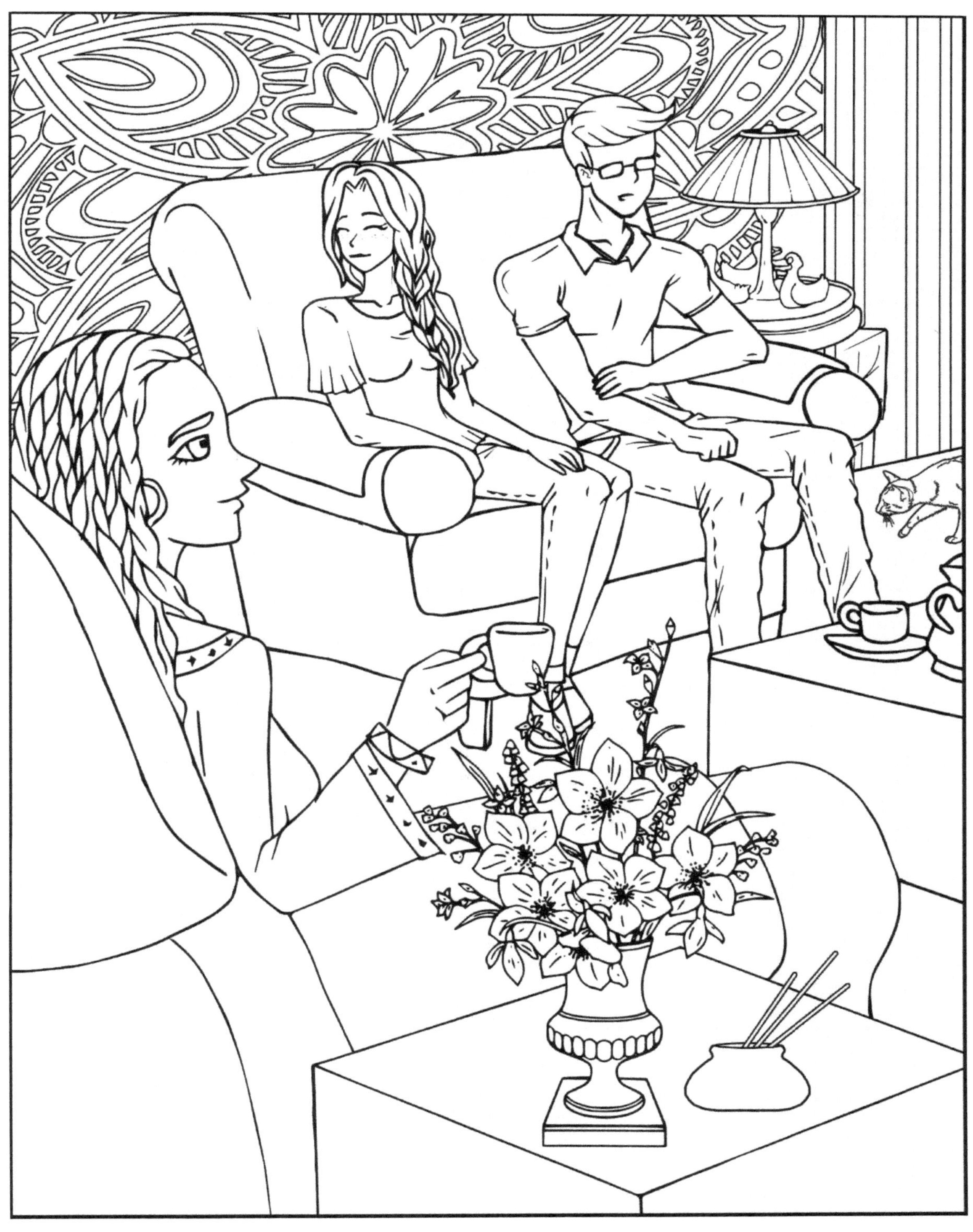

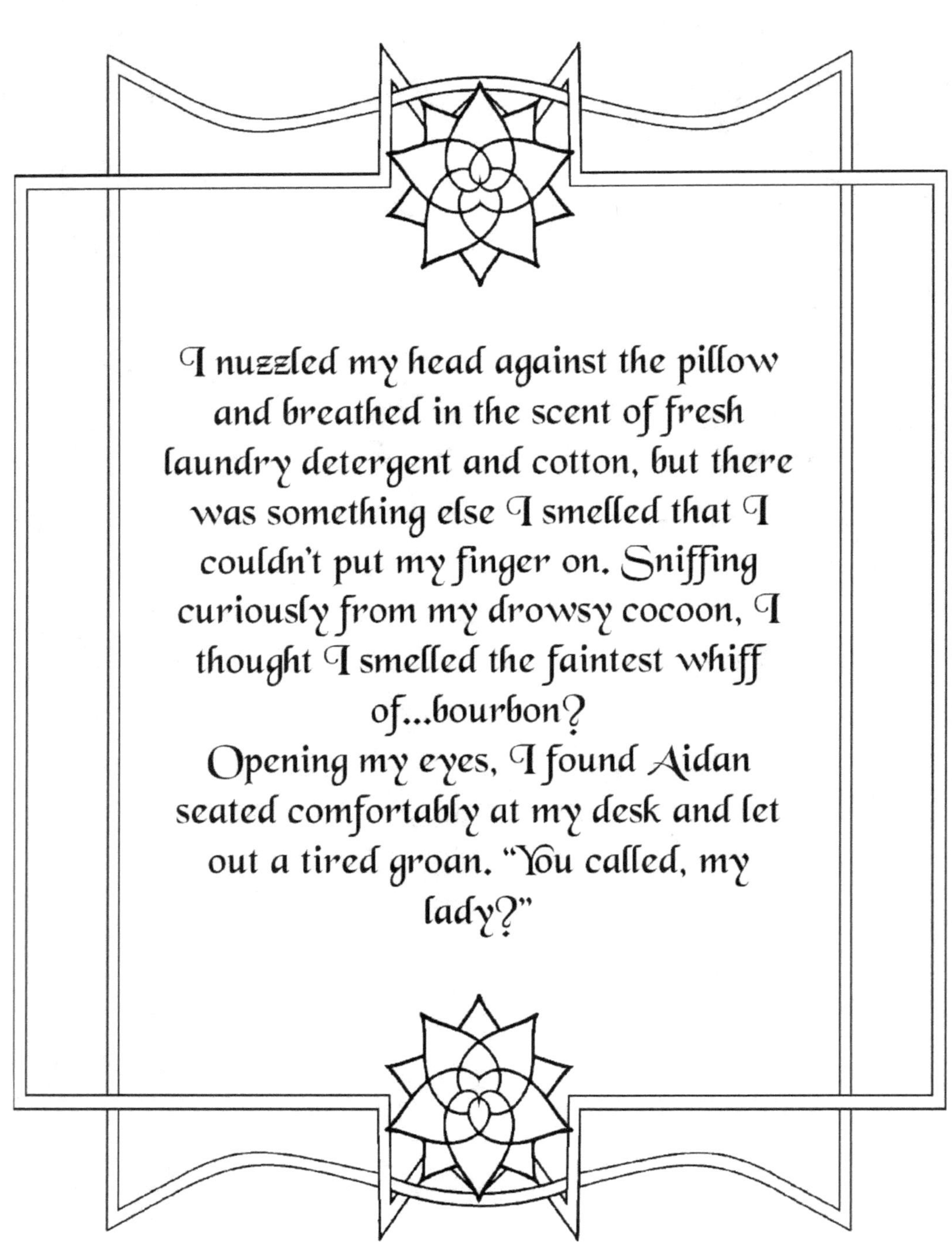

I nuzzled my head against the pillow and breathed in the scent of fresh laundry detergent and cotton, but there was something else I smelled that I couldn't put my finger on. Sniffing curiously from my drowsy cocoon, I thought I smelled the faintest whiff of...bourbon?

Opening my eyes, I found Aidan seated comfortably at my desk and let out a tired groan. "You called, my lady?"

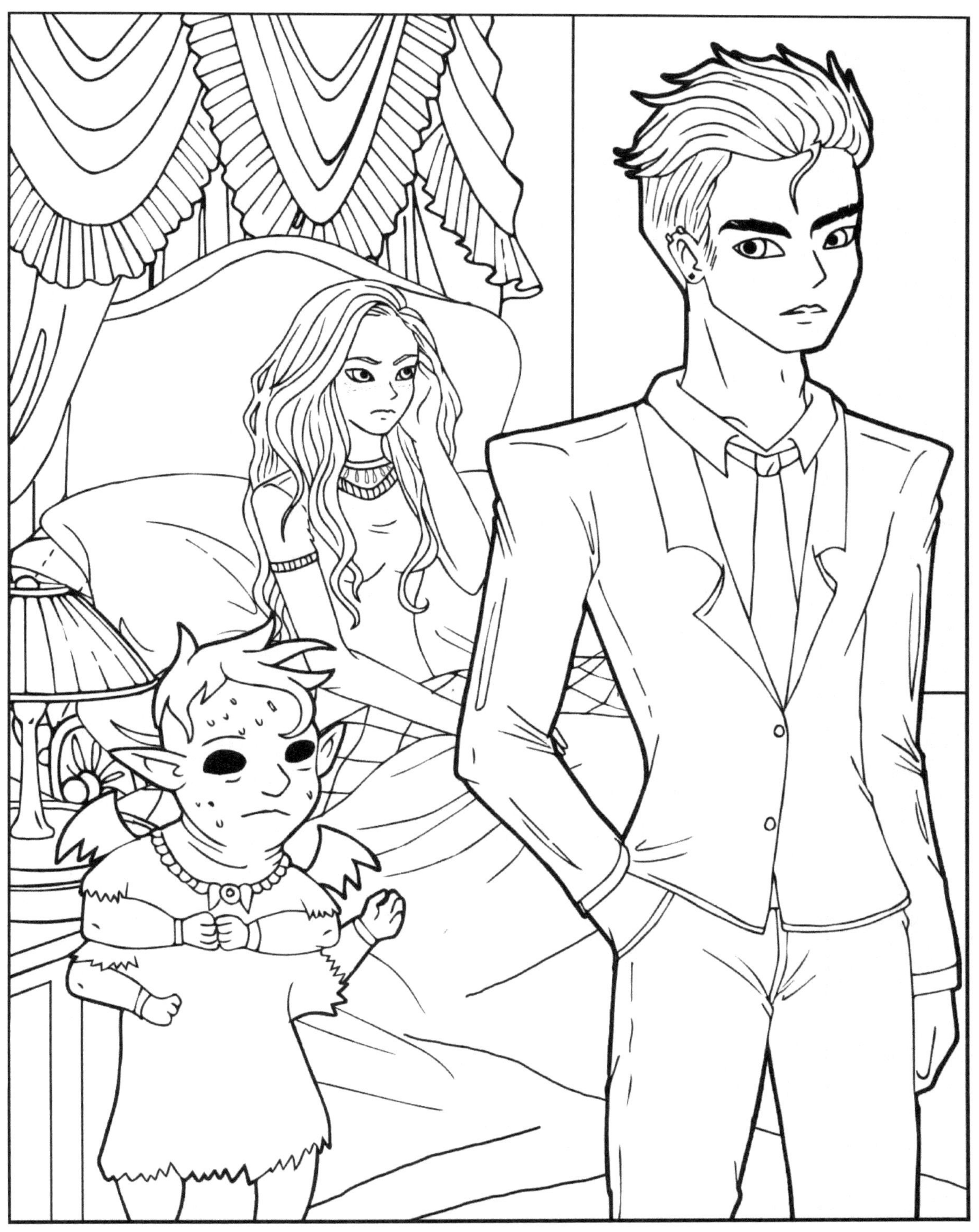

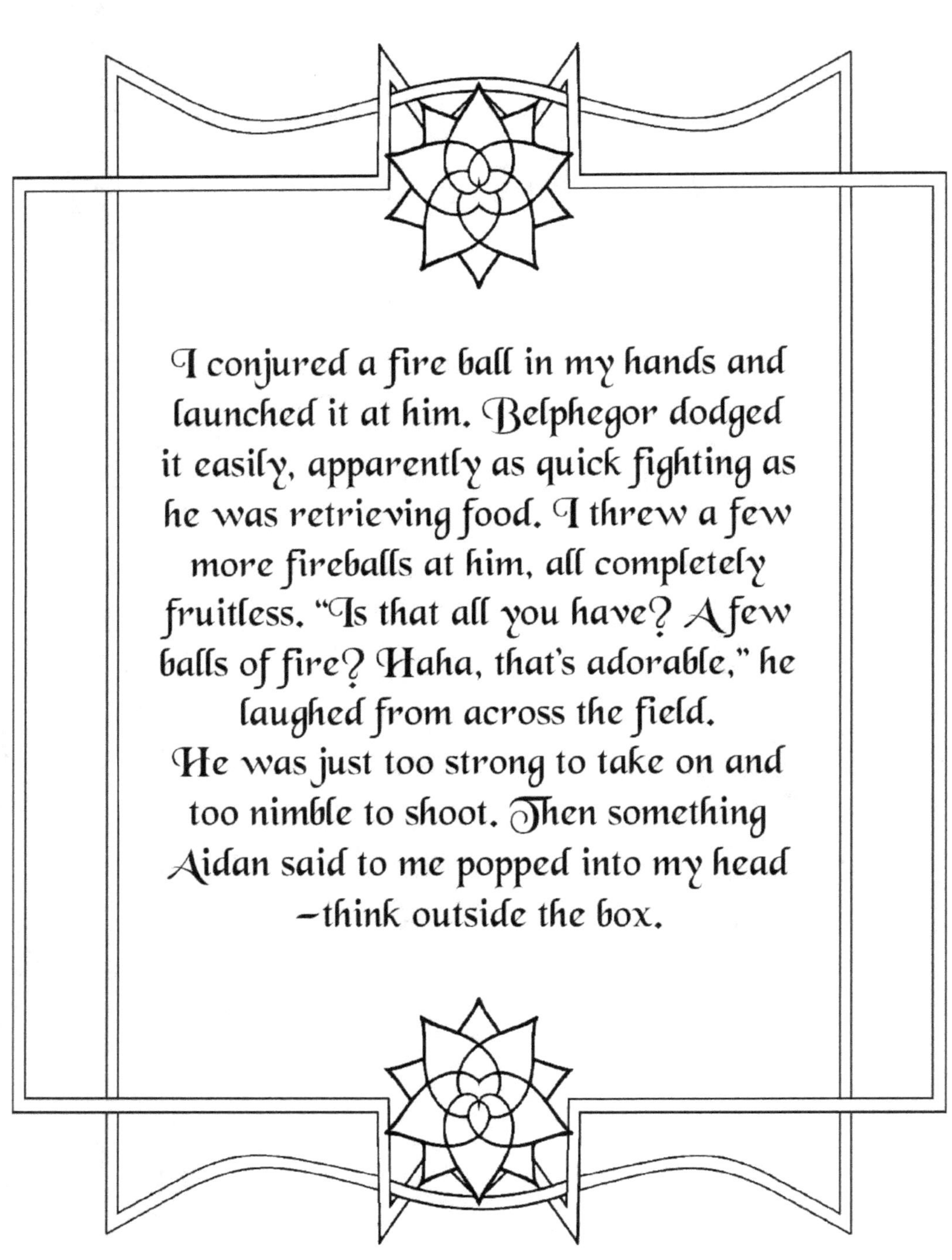

I conjured a fire ball in my hands and launched it at him. Belphegor dodged it easily, apparently as quick fighting as he was retrieving food. I threw a few more fireballs at him, all completely fruitless. "Is that all you have? A few balls of fire? Haha, that's adorable," he laughed from across the field.

He was just too strong to take on and too nimble to shoot. Then something Aidan said to me popped into my head –think outside the box.

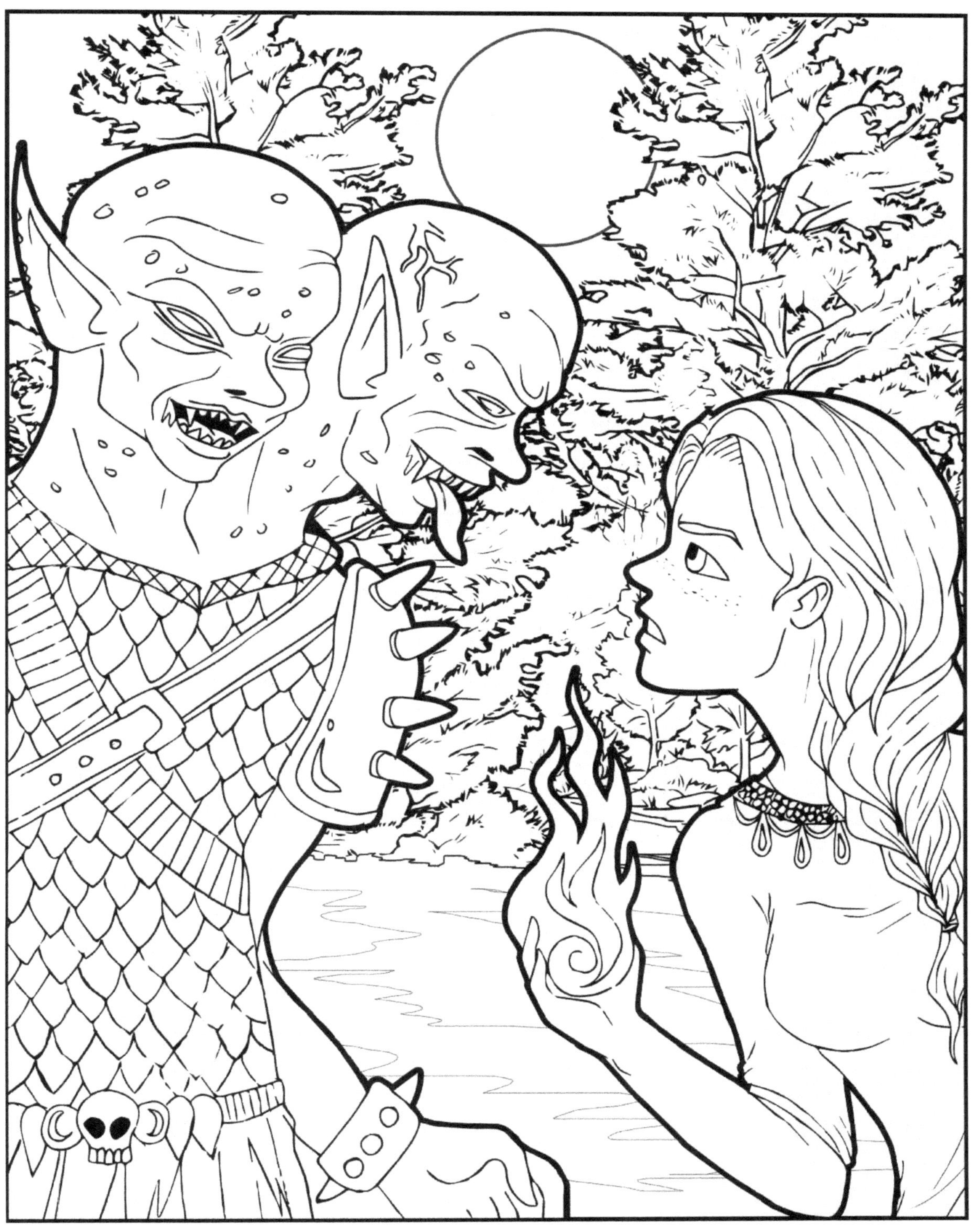

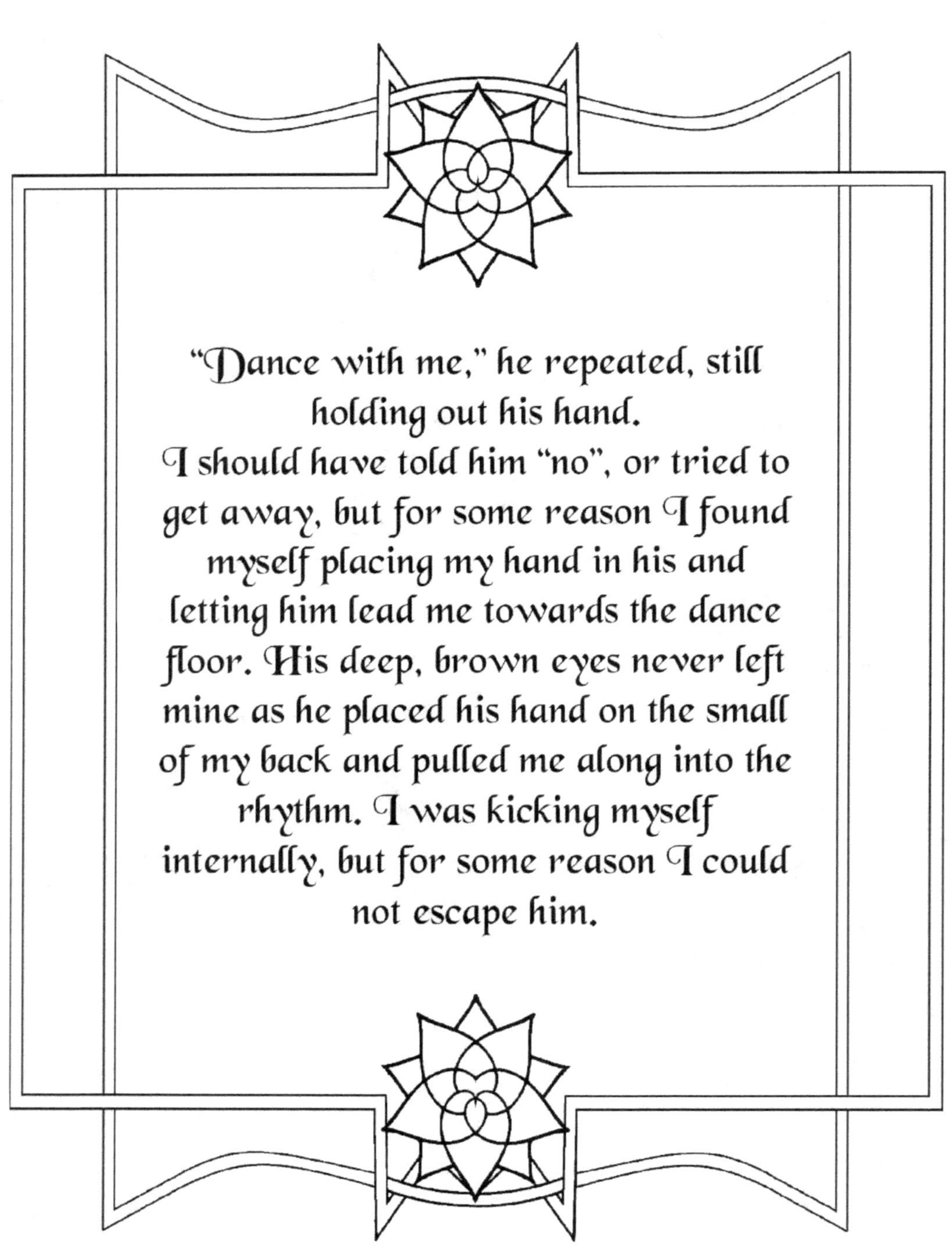

"Dance with me," he repeated, still holding out his hand. I should have told him "no", or tried to get away, but for some reason I found myself placing my hand in his and letting him lead me towards the dance floor. His deep, brown eyes never left mine as he placed his hand on the small of my back and pulled me along into the rhythm. I was kicking myself internally, but for some reason I could not escape him.

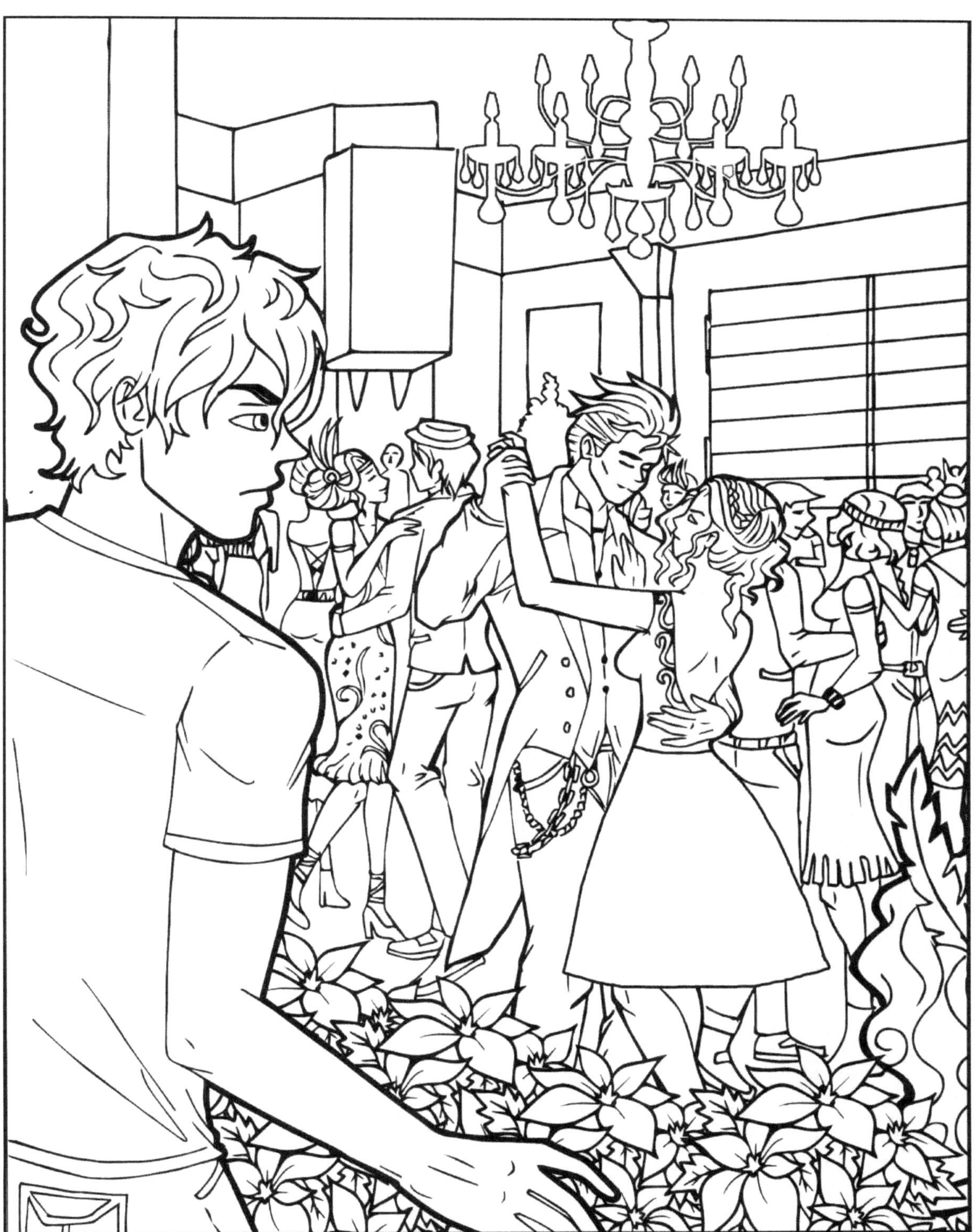

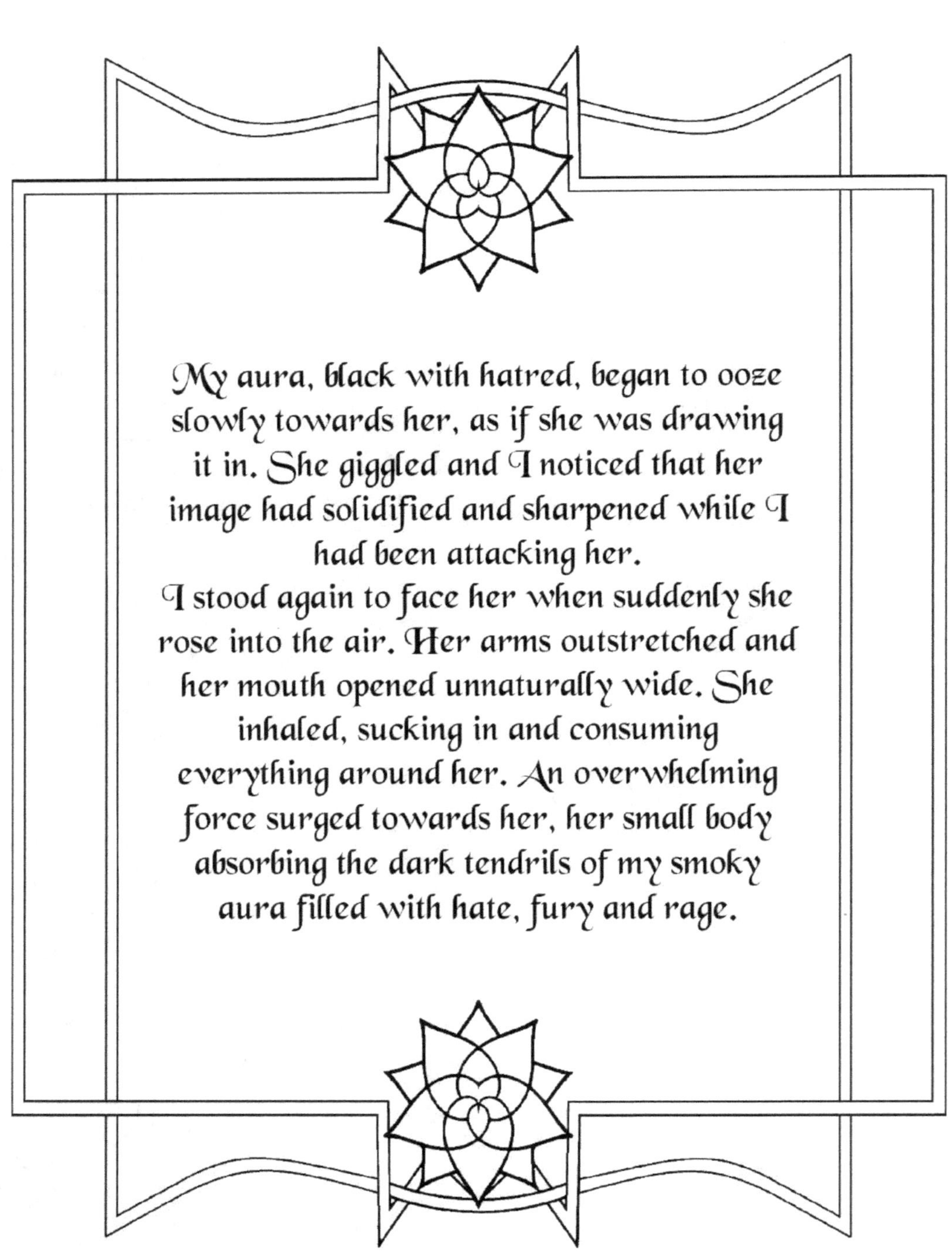

My aura, black with hatred, began to ooze slowly towards her, as if she was drawing it in. She giggled and I noticed that her image had solidified and sharpened while I had been attacking her.

I stood again to face her when suddenly she rose into the air. Her arms outstretched and her mouth opened unnaturally wide. She inhaled, sucking in and consuming everything around her. An overwhelming force surged towards her, her small body absorbing the dark tendrils of my smoky aura filled with hate, fury and rage.

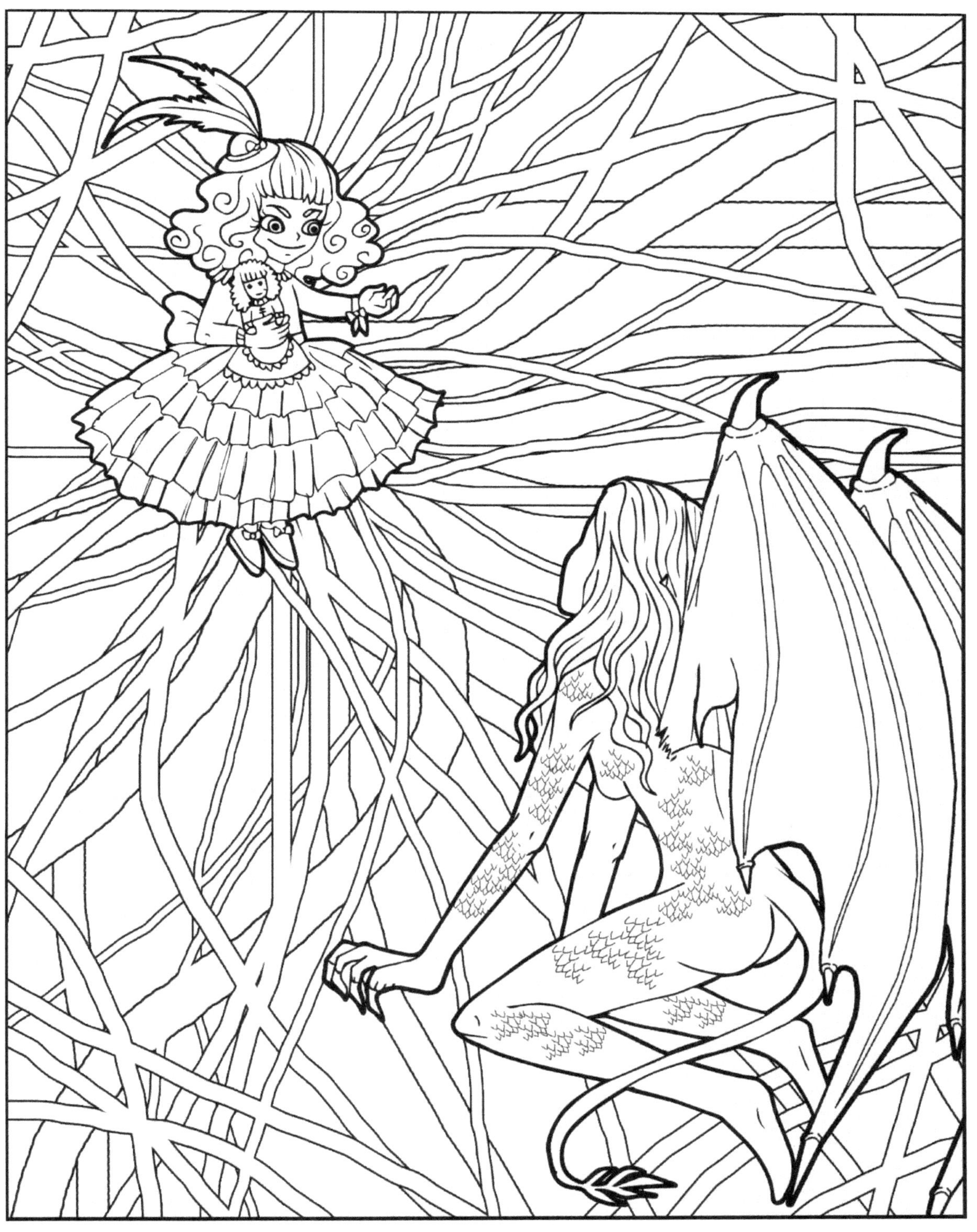

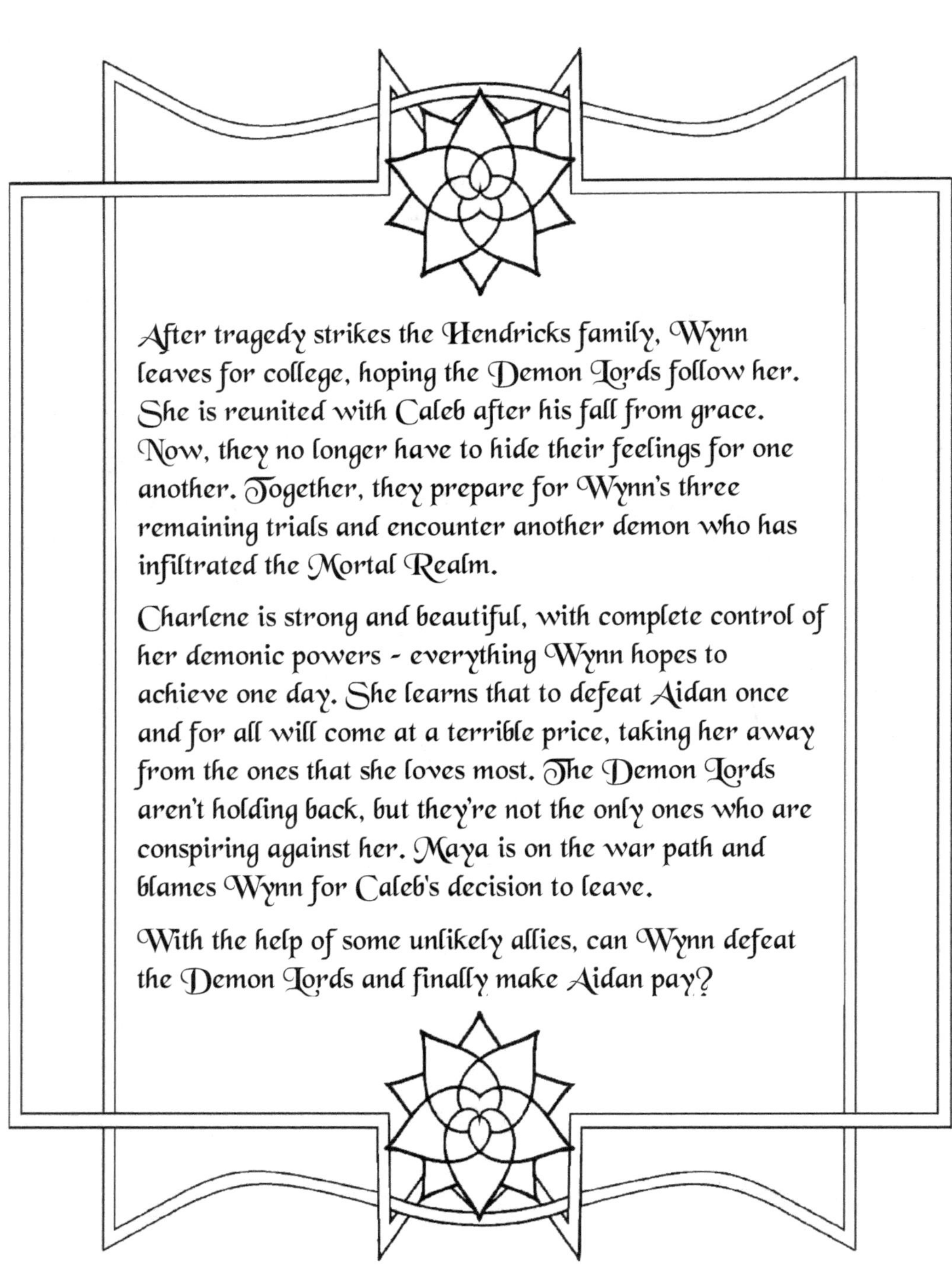

After tragedy strikes the Hendricks family, Wynn leaves for college, hoping the Demon Lords follow her. She is reunited with Caleb after his fall from grace. Now, they no longer have to hide their feelings for one another. Together, they prepare for Wynn's three remaining trials and encounter another demon who has infiltrated the Mortal Realm.

Charlene is strong and beautiful, with complete control of her demonic powers - everything Wynn hopes to achieve one day. She learns that to defeat Aidan once and for all will come at a terrible price, taking her away from the ones that she loves most. The Demon Lords aren't holding back, but they're not the only ones who are conspiring against her. Maya is on the war path and blames Wynn for Caleb's decision to leave.

With the help of some unlikely allies, can Wynn defeat the Demon Lords and finally make Aidan pay?

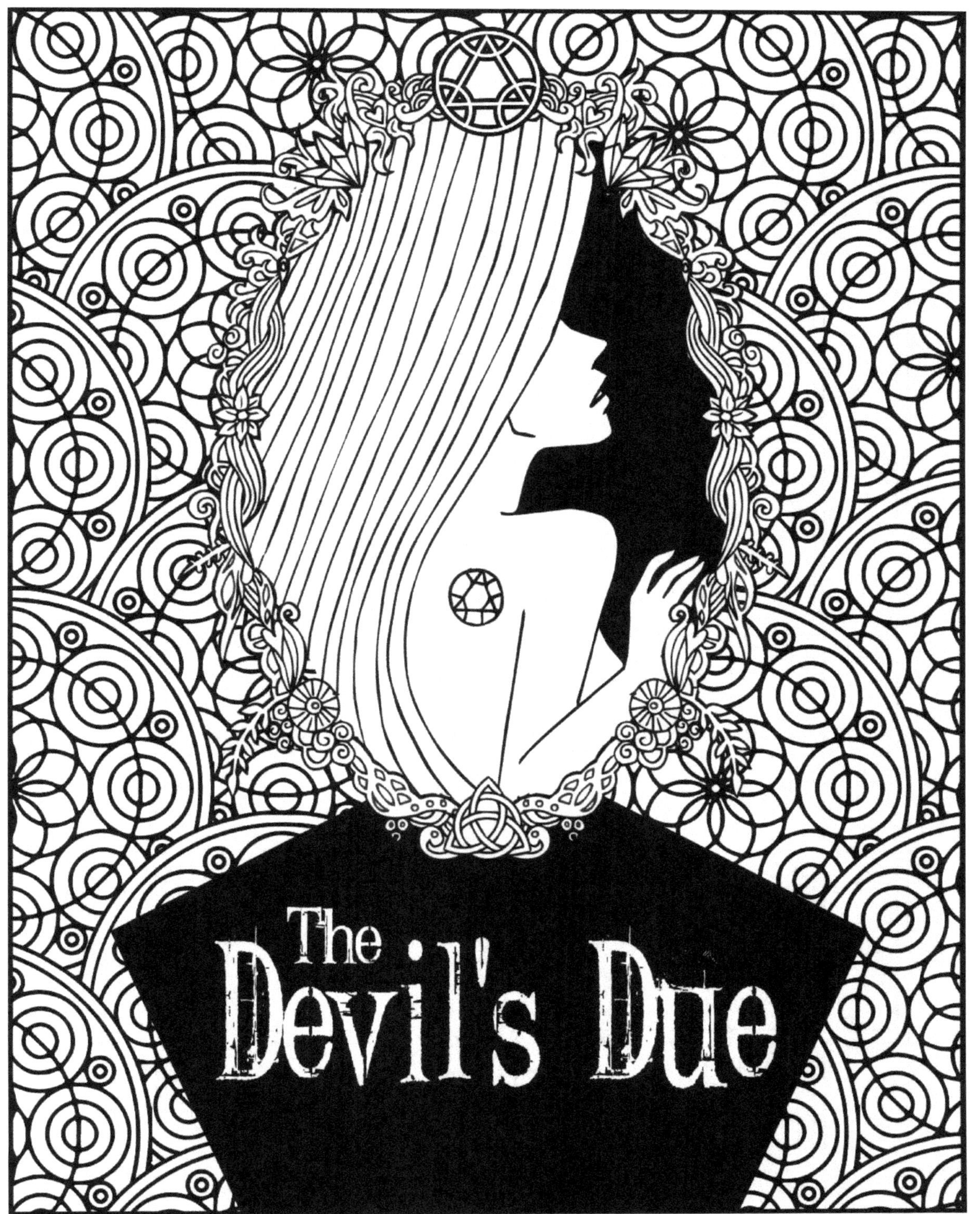
The
Devil's Due

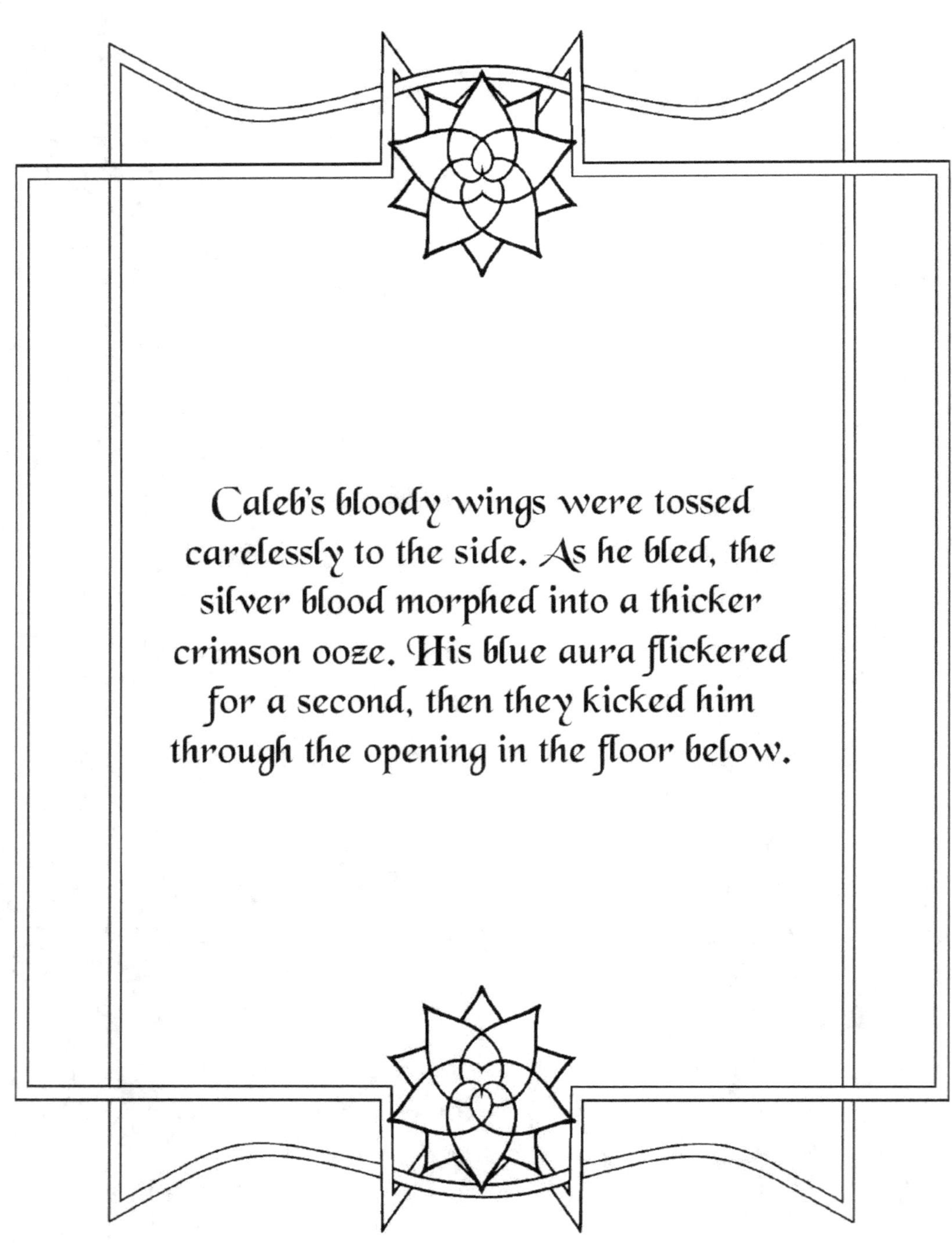

Caleb's bloody wings were tossed carelessly to the side. As he bled, the silver blood morphed into a thicker crimson ooze. His blue aura flickered for a second, then they kicked him through the opening in the floor below.

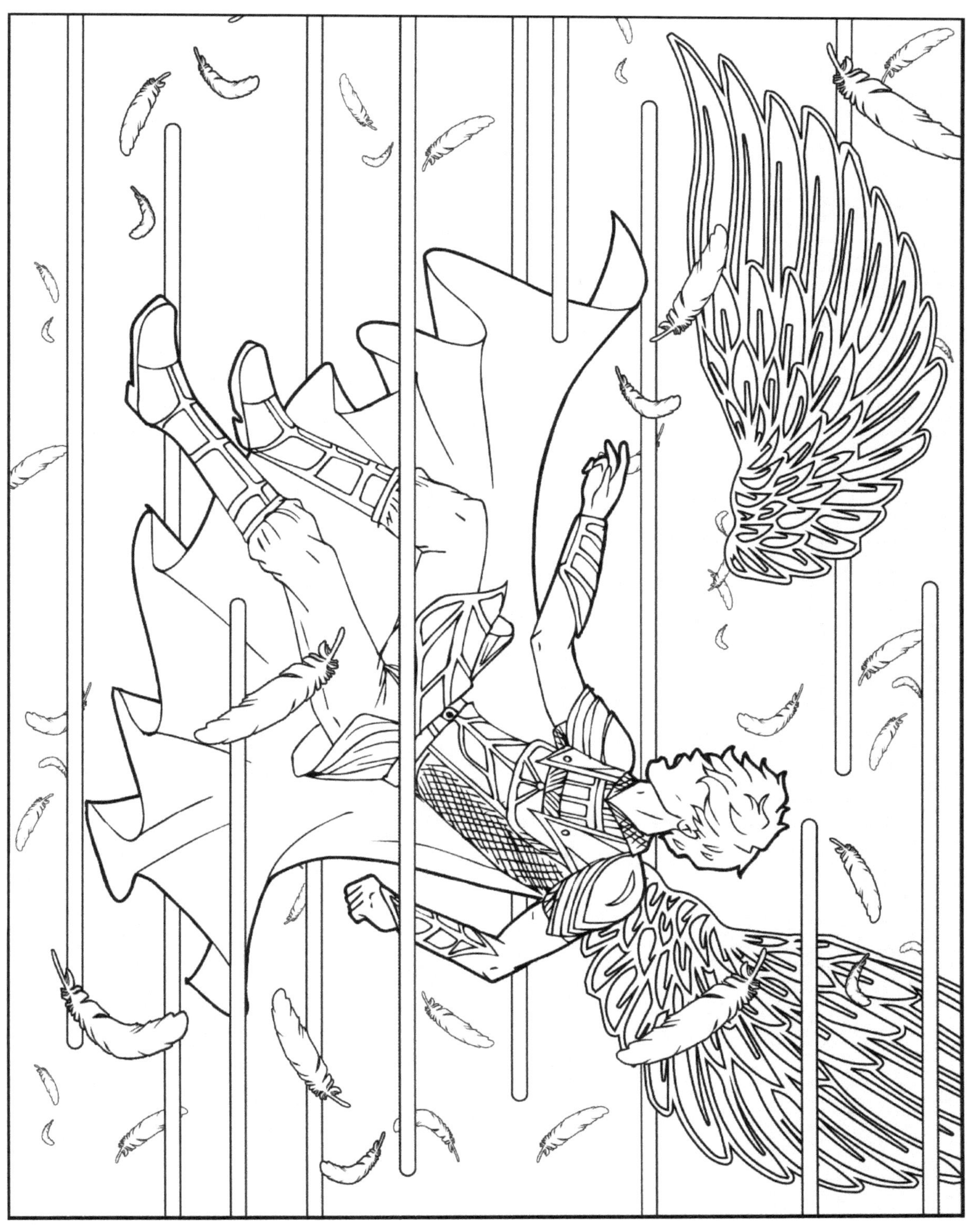

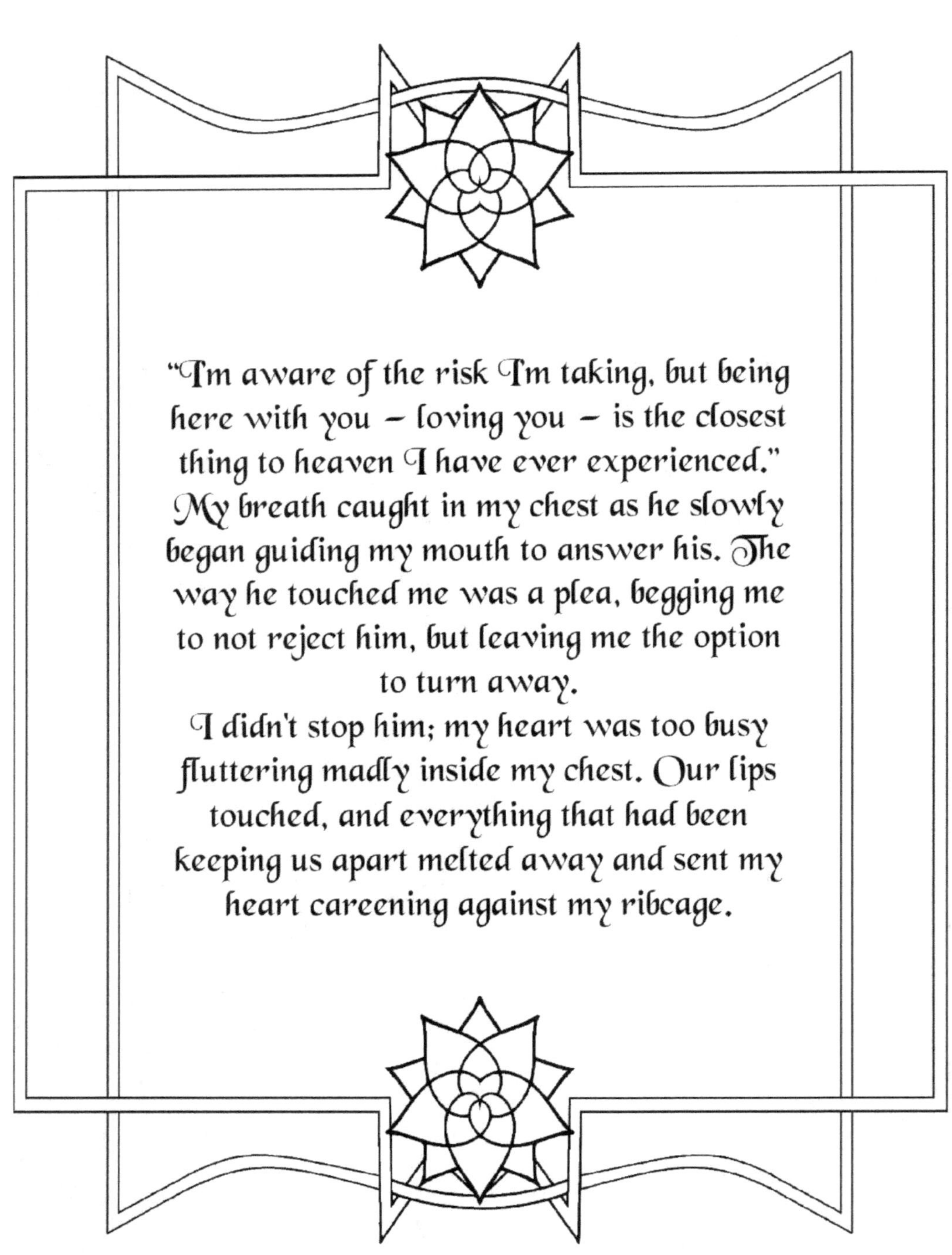

"I'm aware of the risk I'm taking, but being here with you – loving you – is the closest thing to heaven I have ever experienced."

My breath caught in my chest as he slowly began guiding my mouth to answer his. The way he touched me was a plea, begging me to not reject him, but leaving me the option to turn away.

I didn't stop him; my heart was too busy fluttering madly inside my chest. Our lips touched, and everything that had been keeping us apart melted away and sent my heart careening against my ribcage.

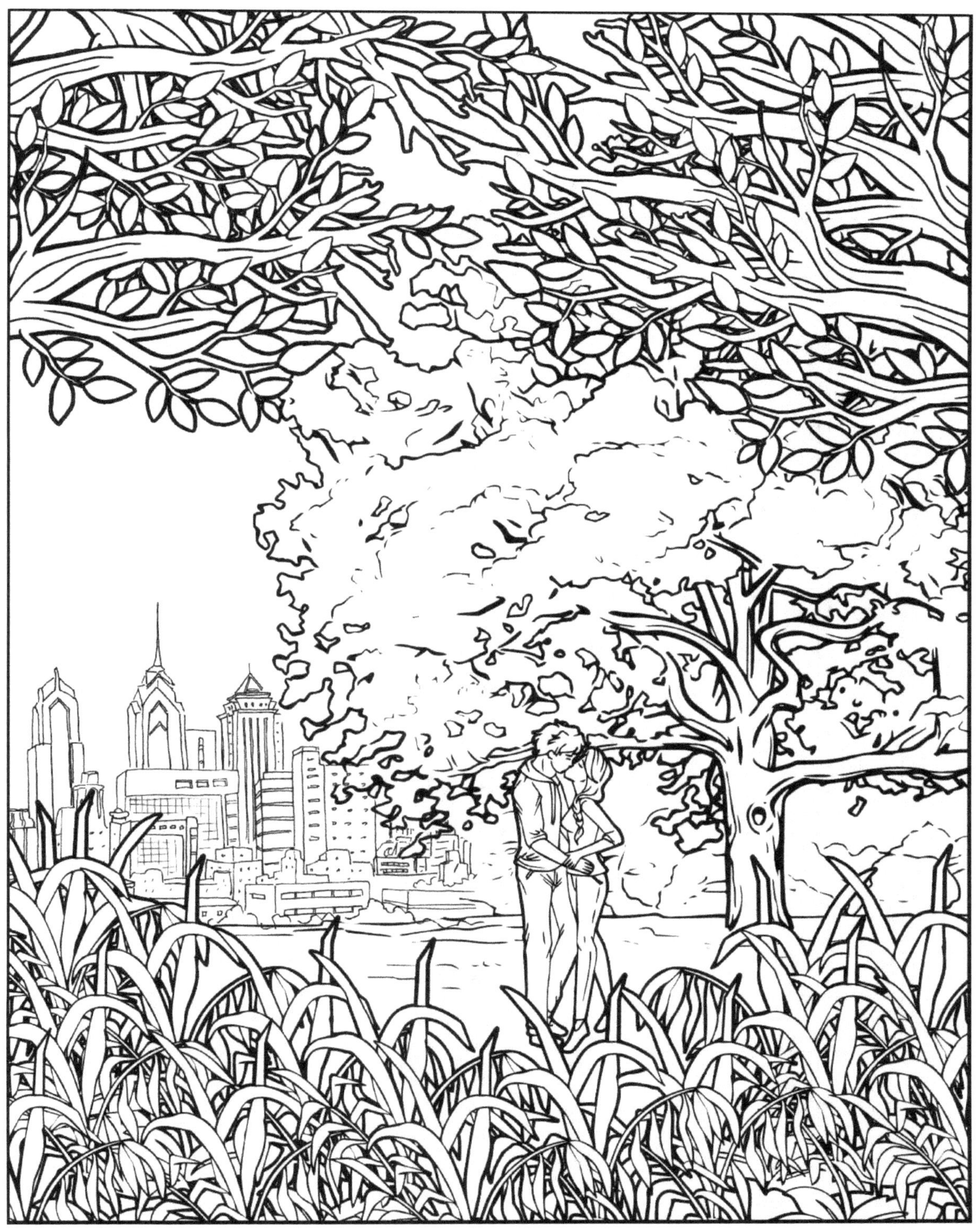

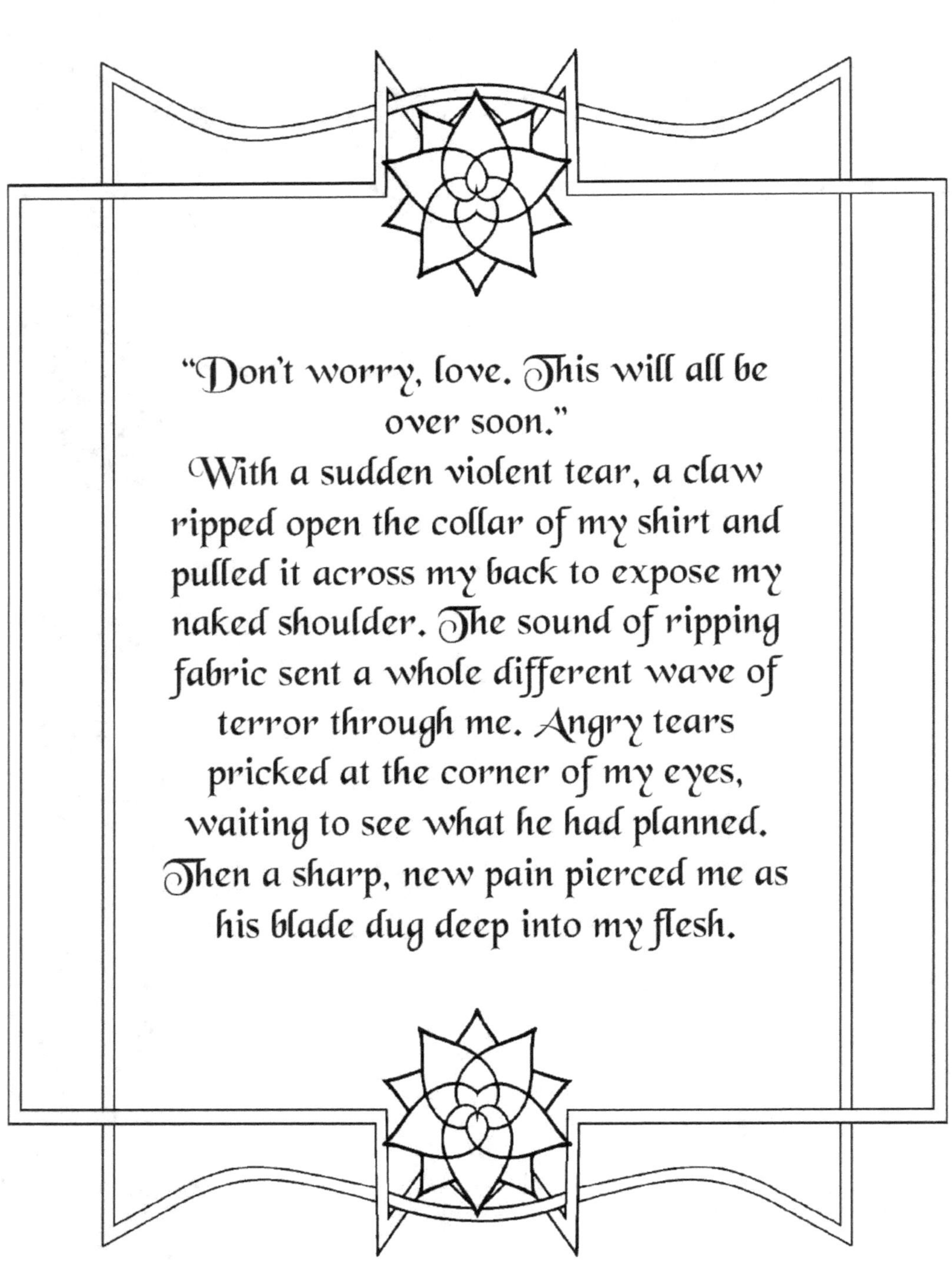

"Don't worry, love. This will all be over soon."

With a sudden violent tear, a claw ripped open the collar of my shirt and pulled it across my back to expose my naked shoulder. The sound of ripping fabric sent a whole different wave of terror through me. Angry tears pricked at the corner of my eyes, waiting to see what he had planned. Then a sharp, new pain pierced me as his blade dug deep into my flesh.

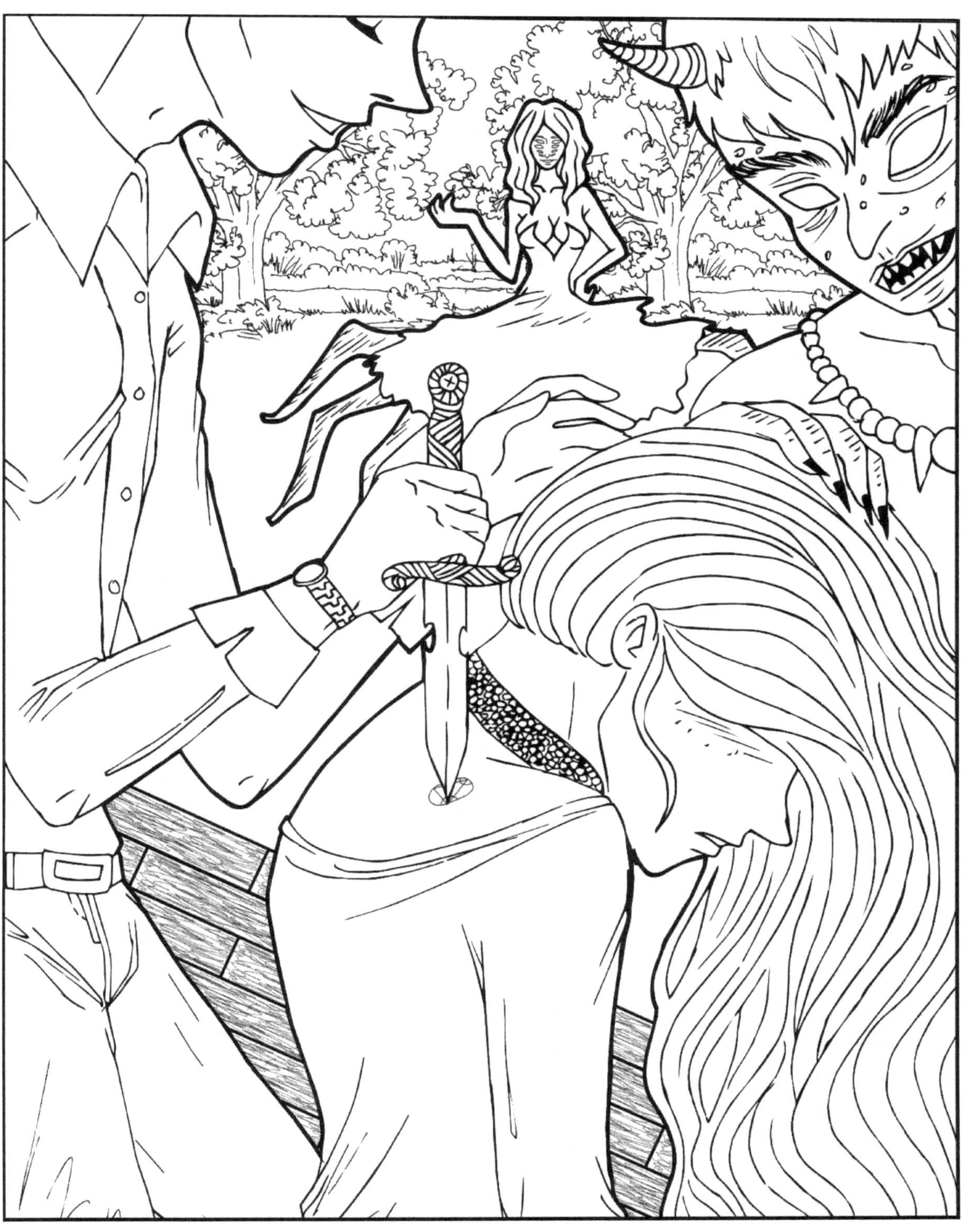

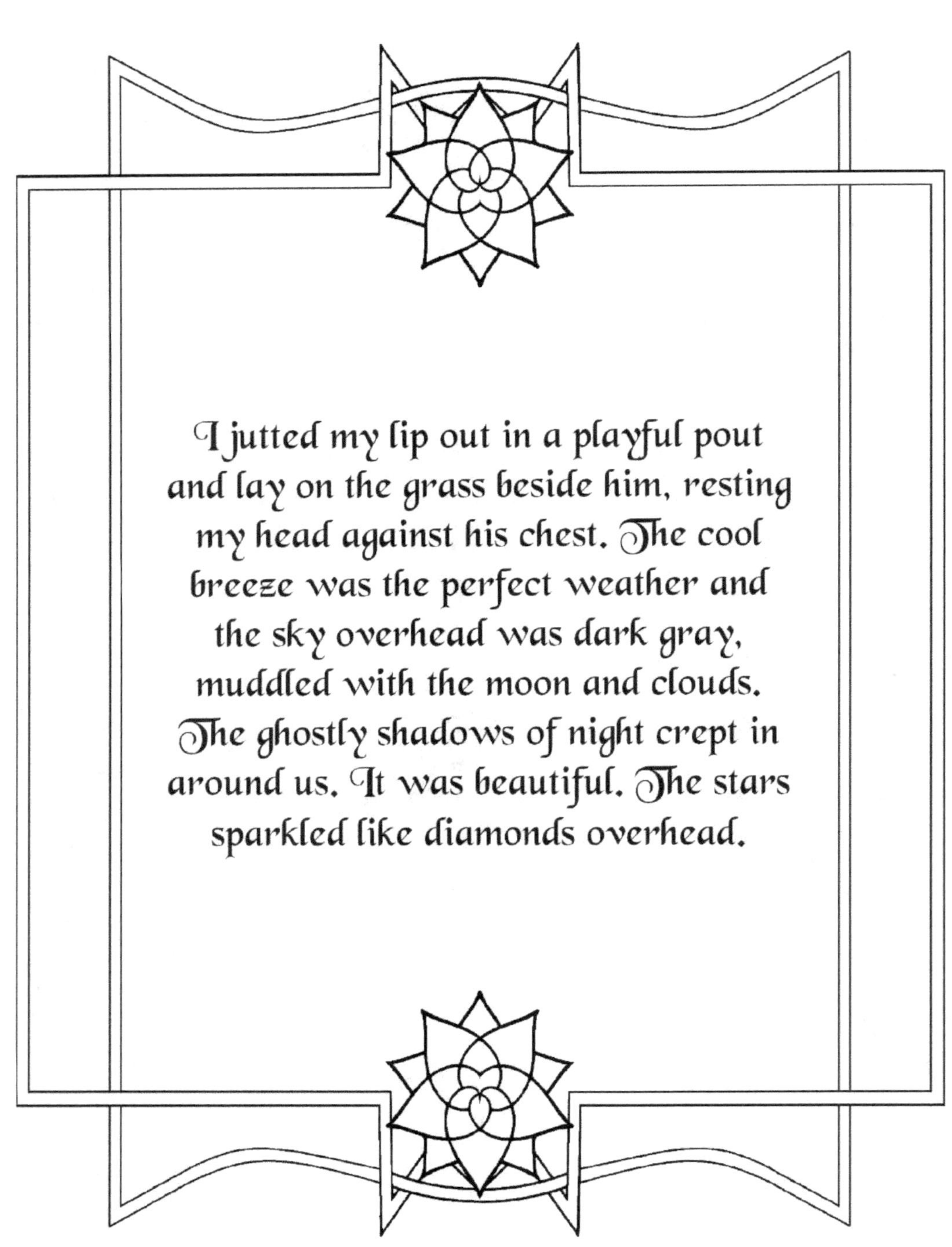

I jutted my lip out in a playful pout and lay on the grass beside him, resting my head against his chest. The cool breeze was the perfect weather and the sky overhead was dark gray, muddled with the moon and clouds. The ghostly shadows of night crept in around us. It was beautiful. The stars sparkled like diamonds overhead.

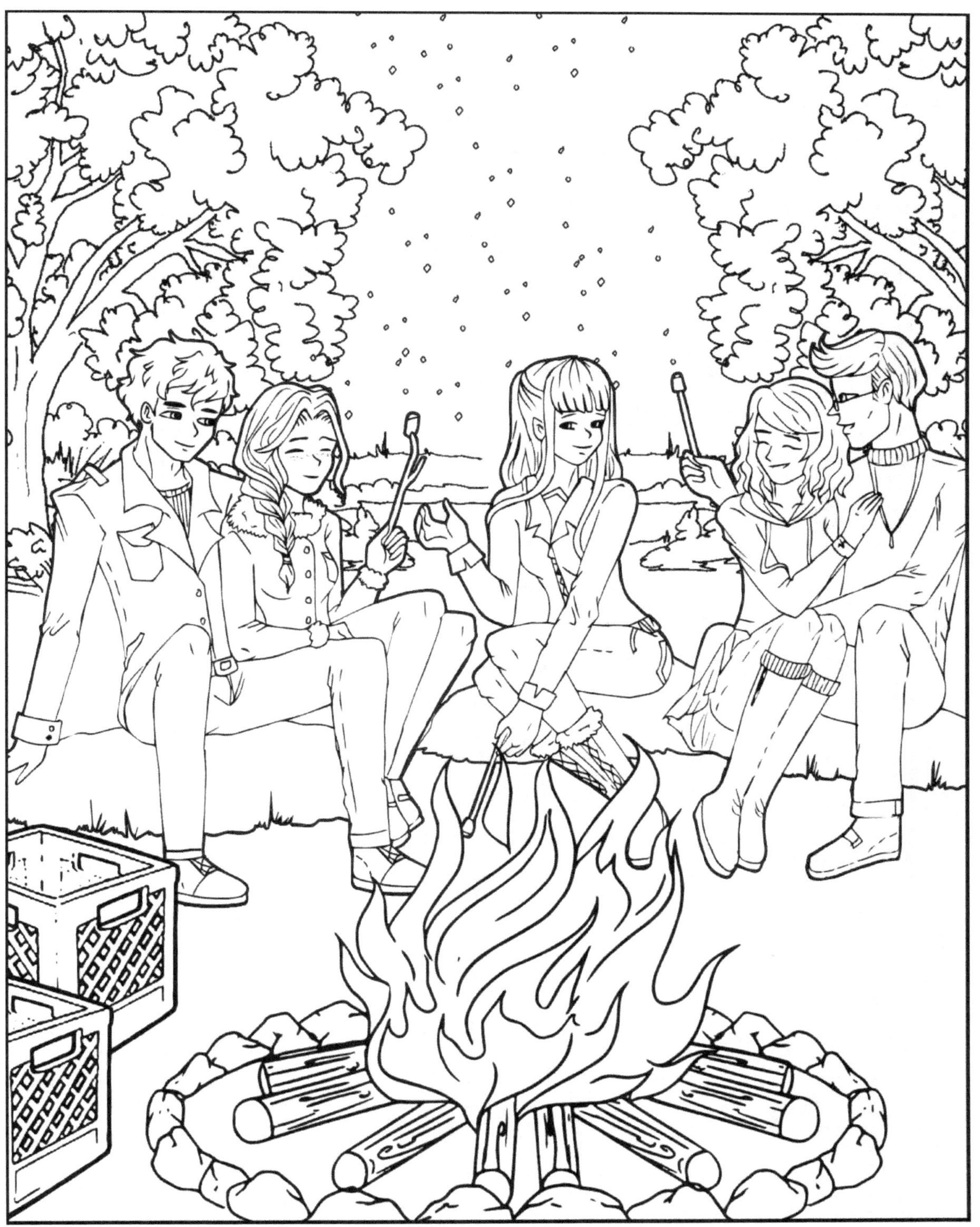

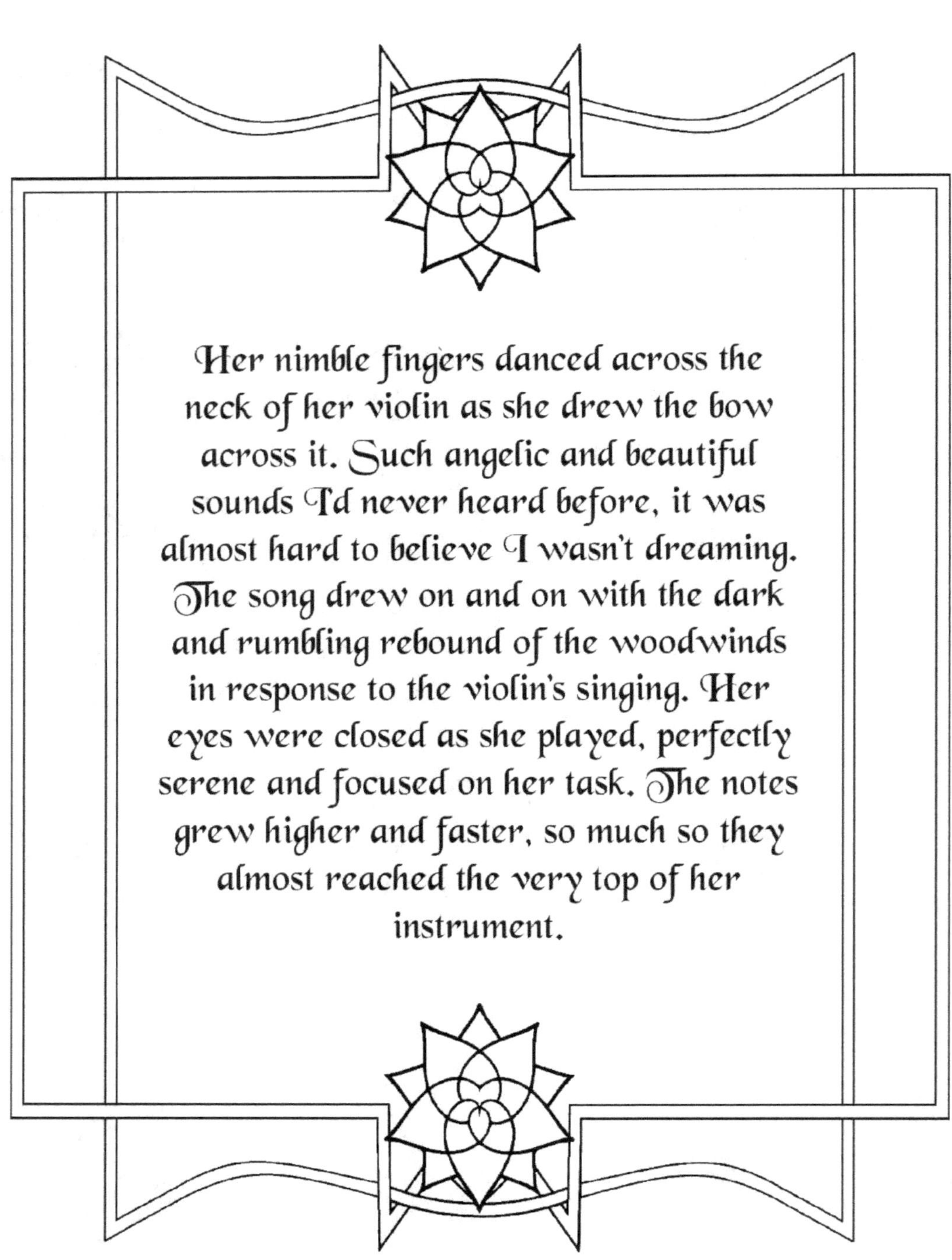

Her nimble fingers danced across the neck of her violin as she drew the bow across it. Such angelic and beautiful sounds I'd never heard before, it was almost hard to believe I wasn't dreaming. The song drew on and on with the dark and rumbling rebound of the woodwinds in response to the violin's singing. Her eyes were closed as she played, perfectly serene and focused on her task. The notes grew higher and faster, so much so they almost reached the very top of her instrument.

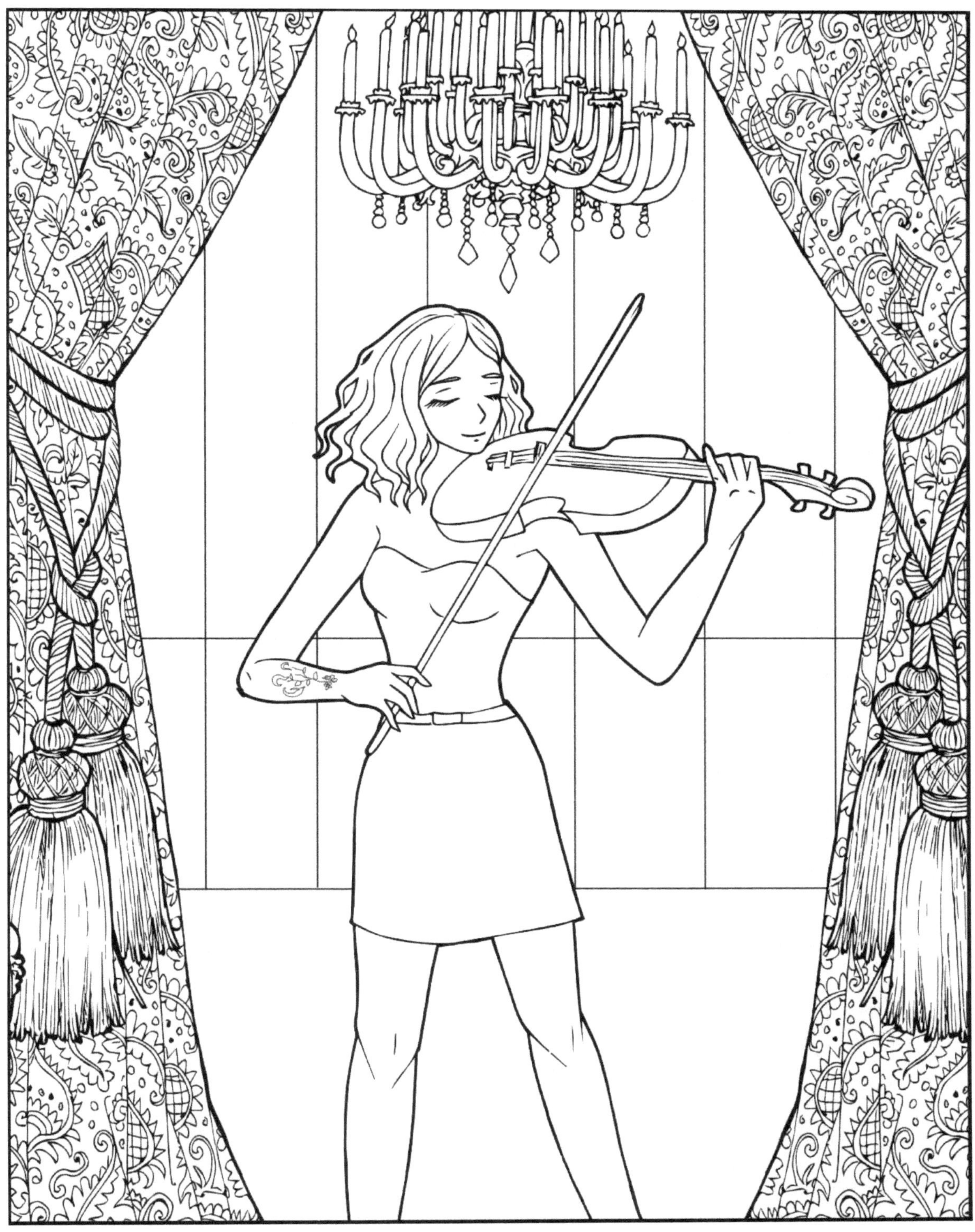

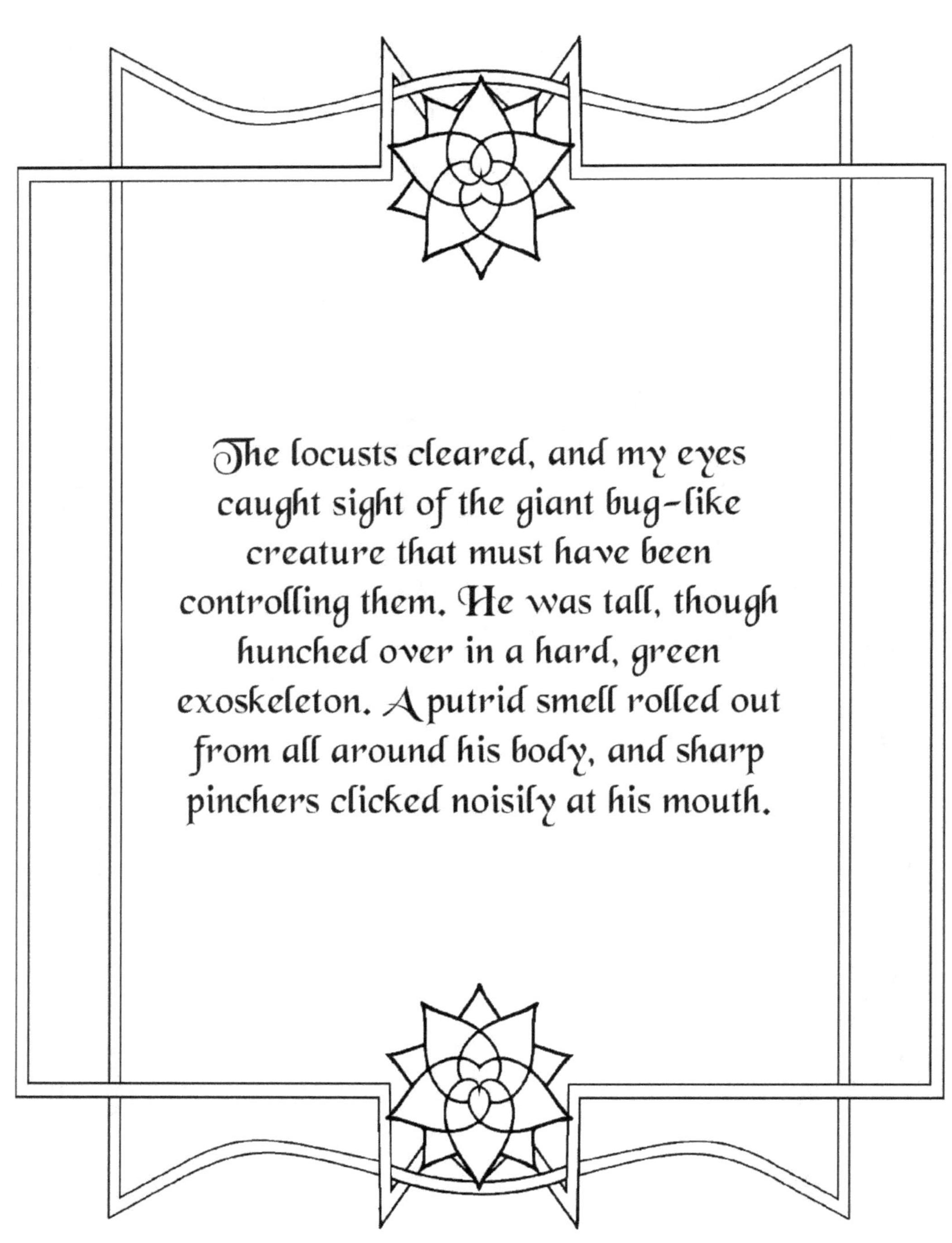

The locusts cleared, and my eyes caught sight of the giant bug-like creature that must have been controlling them. He was tall, though hunched over in a hard, green exoskeleton. A putrid smell rolled out from all around his body, and sharp pinchers clicked noisily at his mouth.

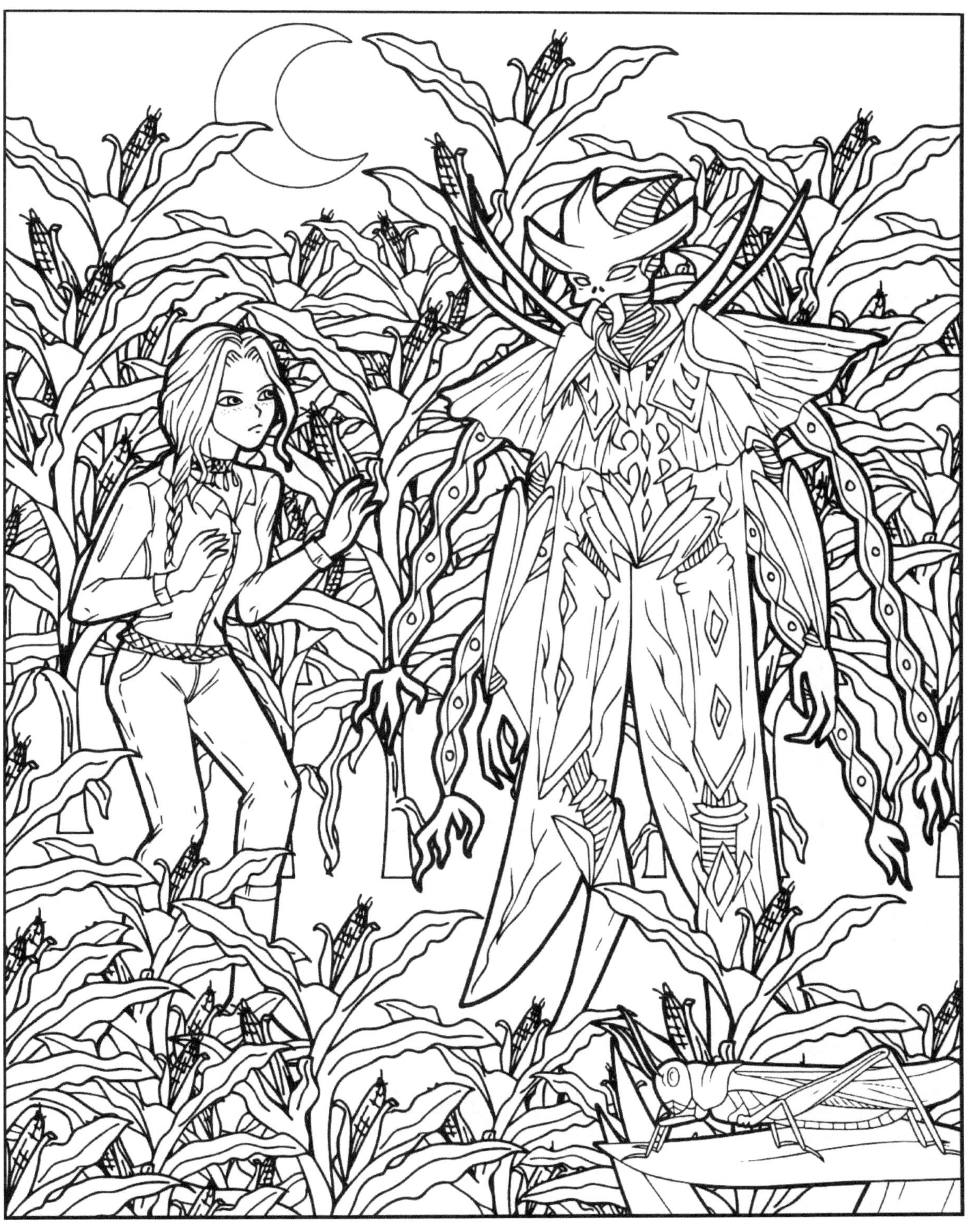

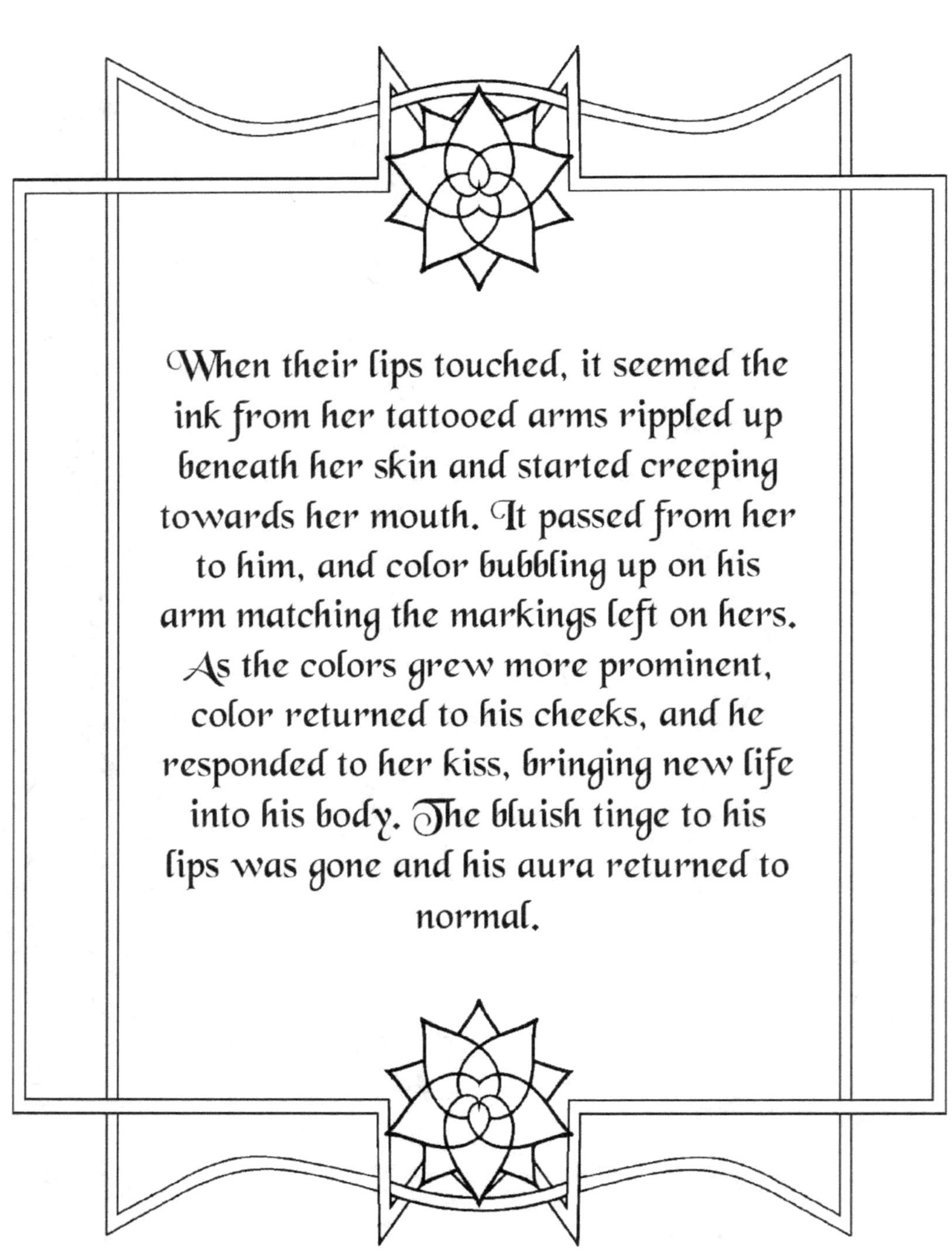

When their lips touched, it seemed the ink from her tattooed arms rippled up beneath her skin and started creeping towards her mouth. It passed from her to him, and color bubbling up on his arm matching the markings left on hers. As the colors grew more prominent, color returned to his cheeks, and he responded to her kiss, bringing new life into his body. The bluish tinge to his lips was gone and his aura returned to normal.

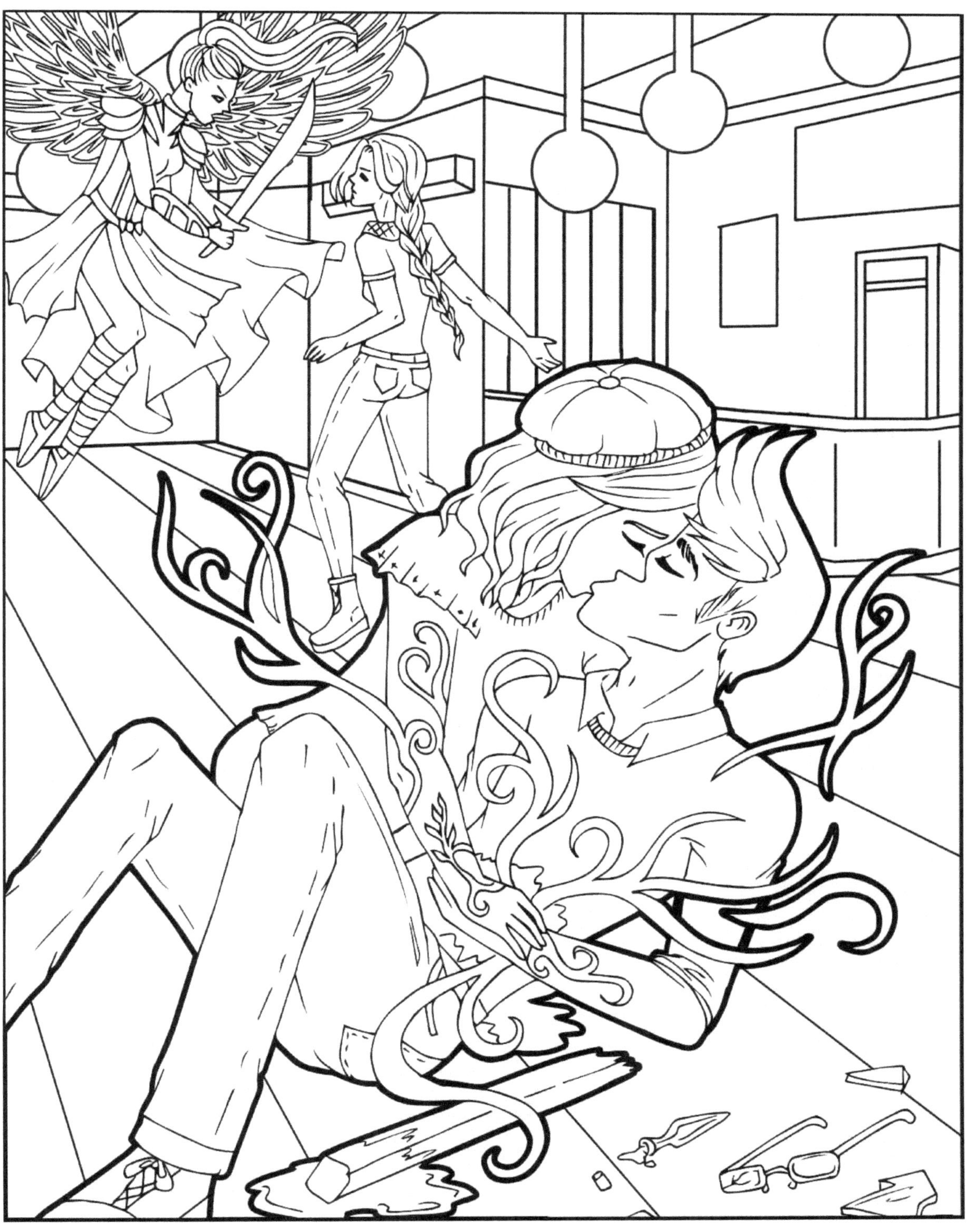

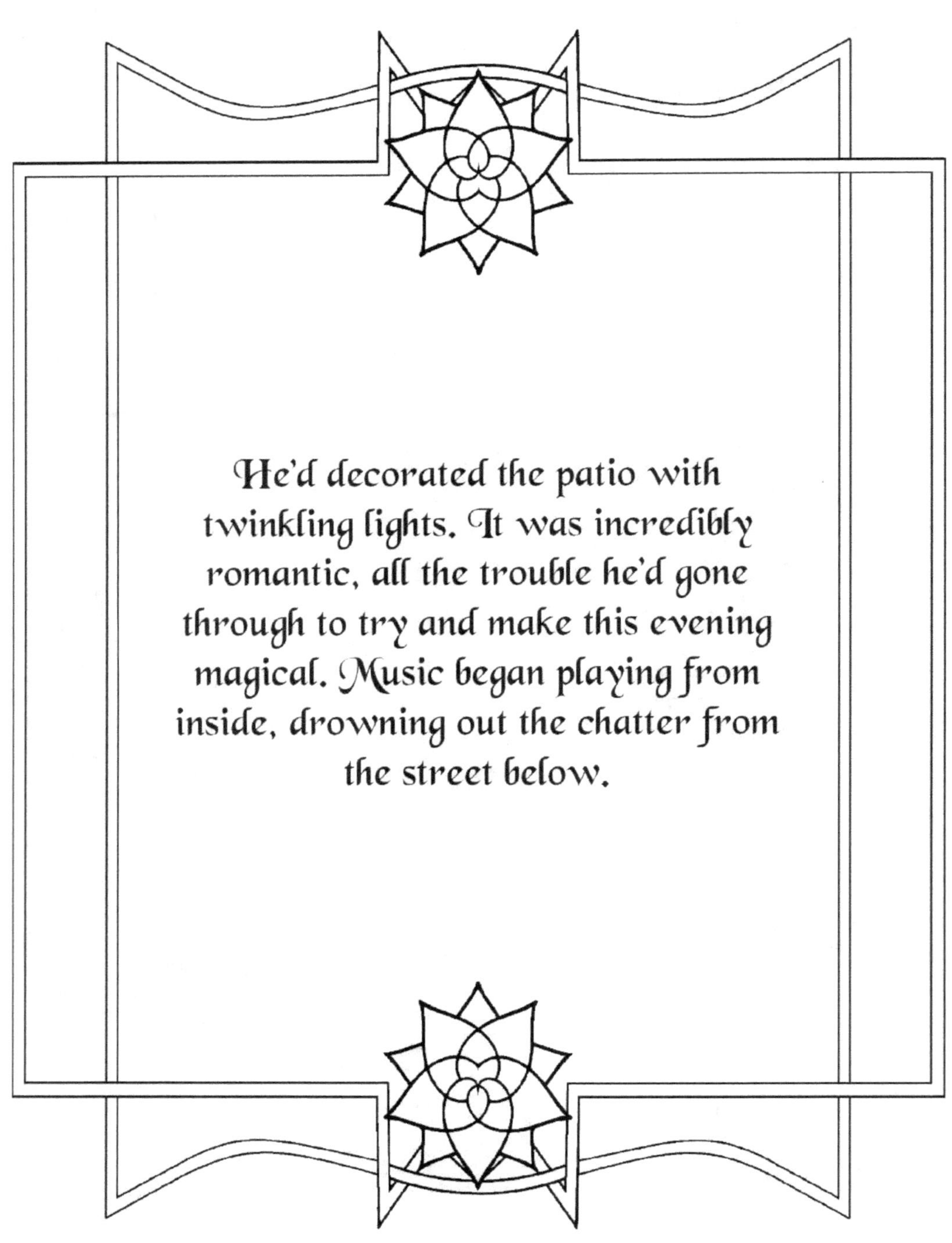

He'd decorated the patio with twinkling lights. It was incredibly romantic, all the trouble he'd gone through to try and make this evening magical. Music began playing from inside, drowning out the chatter from the street below.

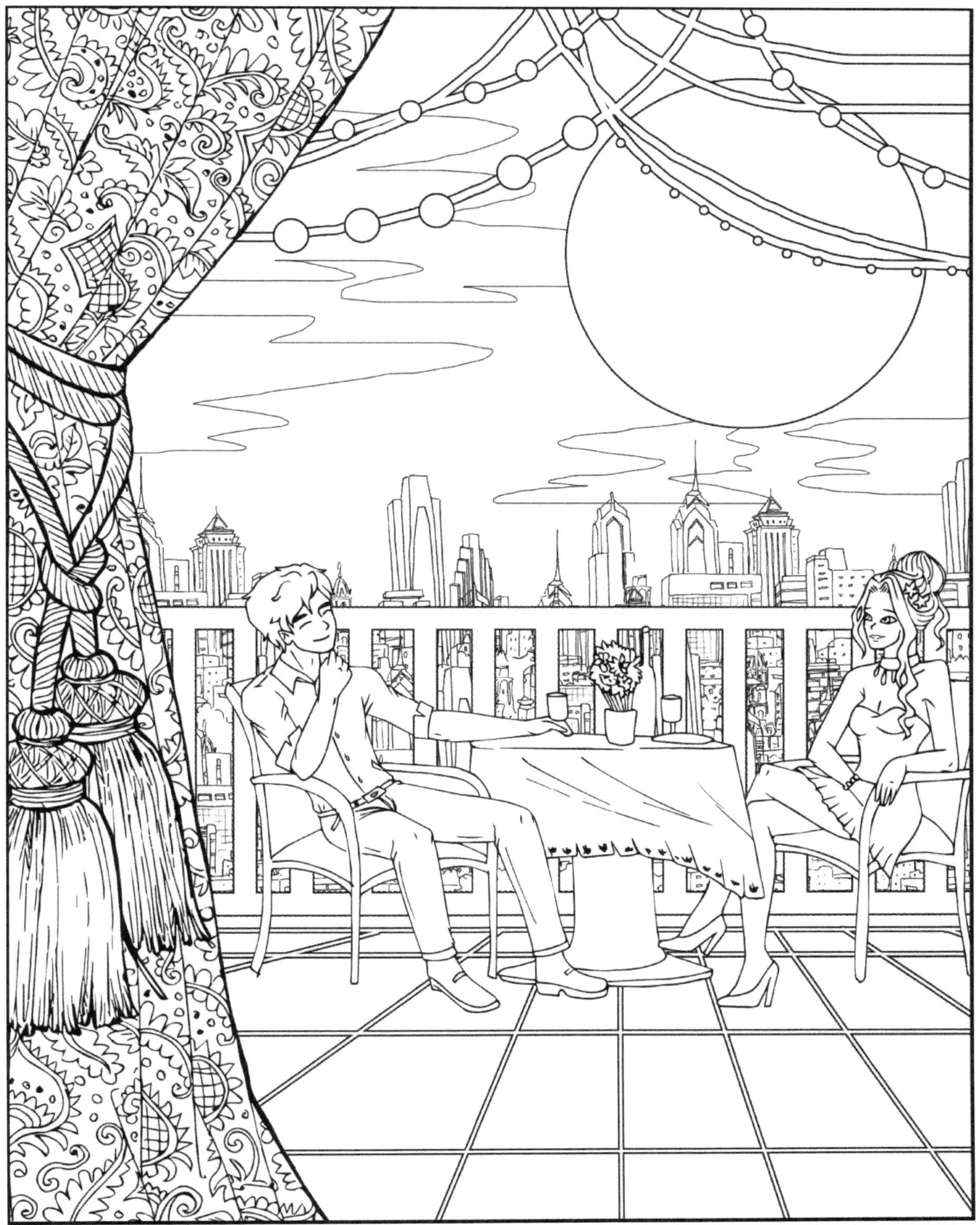

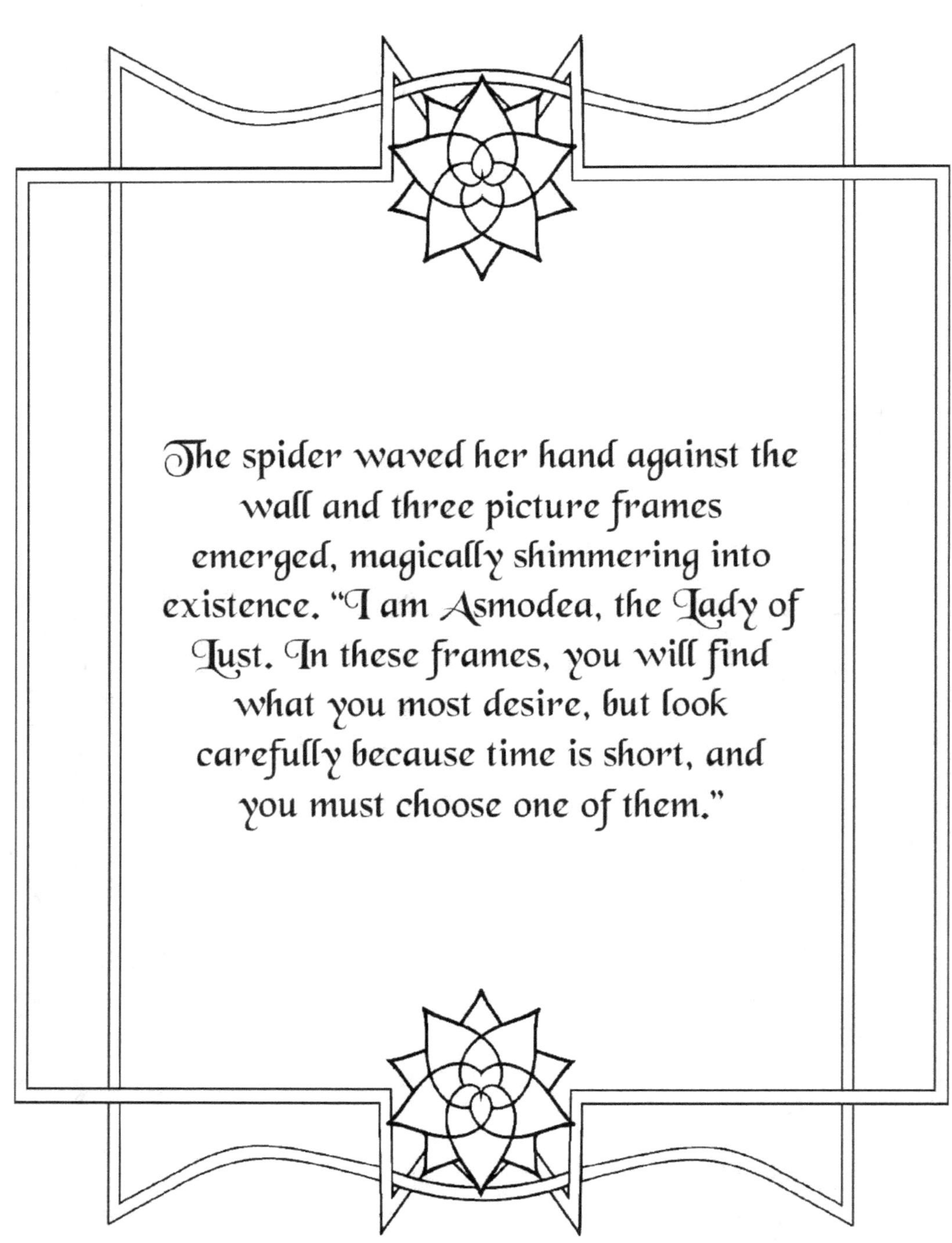

The spider waved her hand against the wall and three picture frames emerged, magically shimmering into existence. "I am Asmodea, the Lady of Lust. In these frames, you will find what you most desire, but look carefully because time is short, and you must choose one of them."

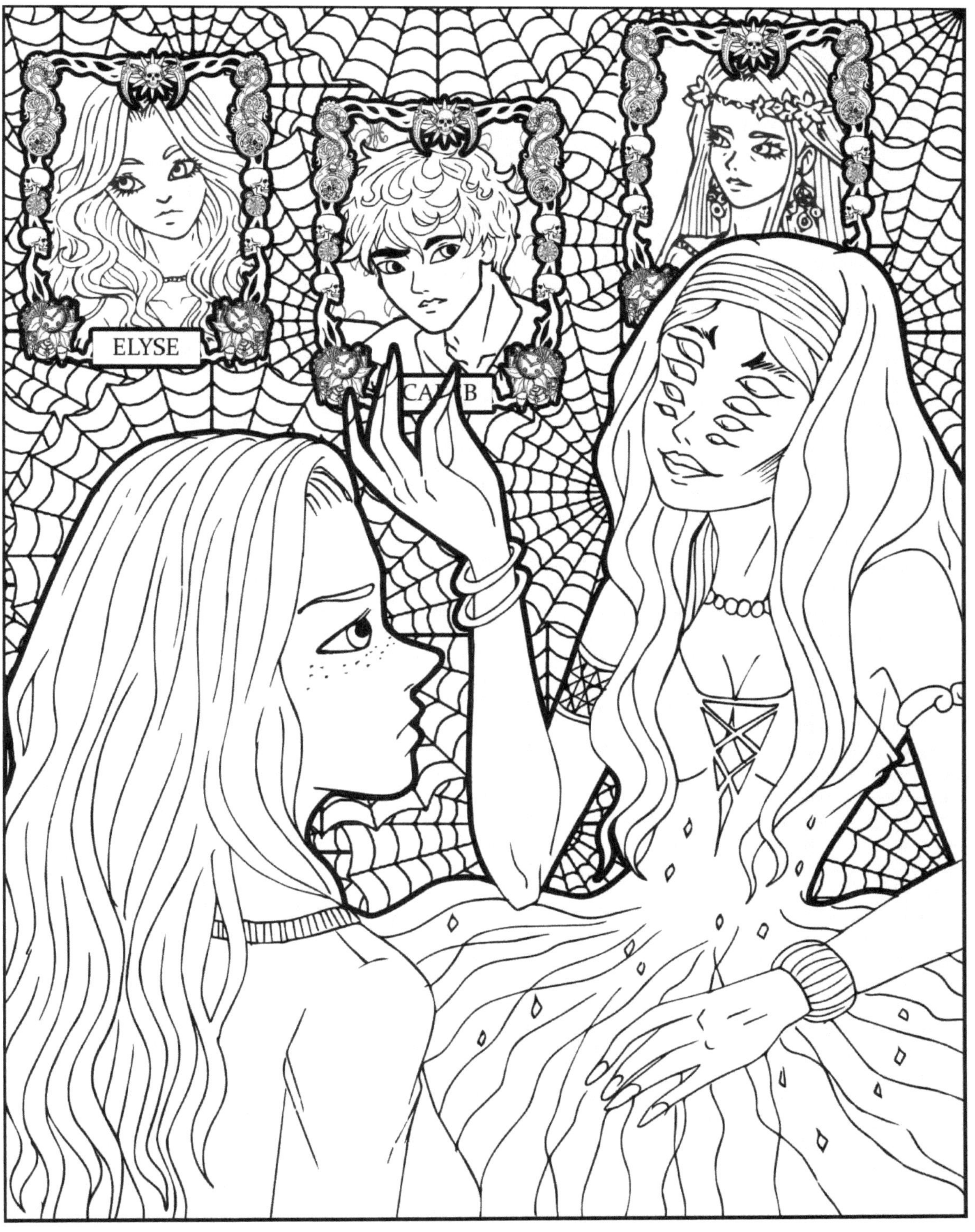
ELYSE

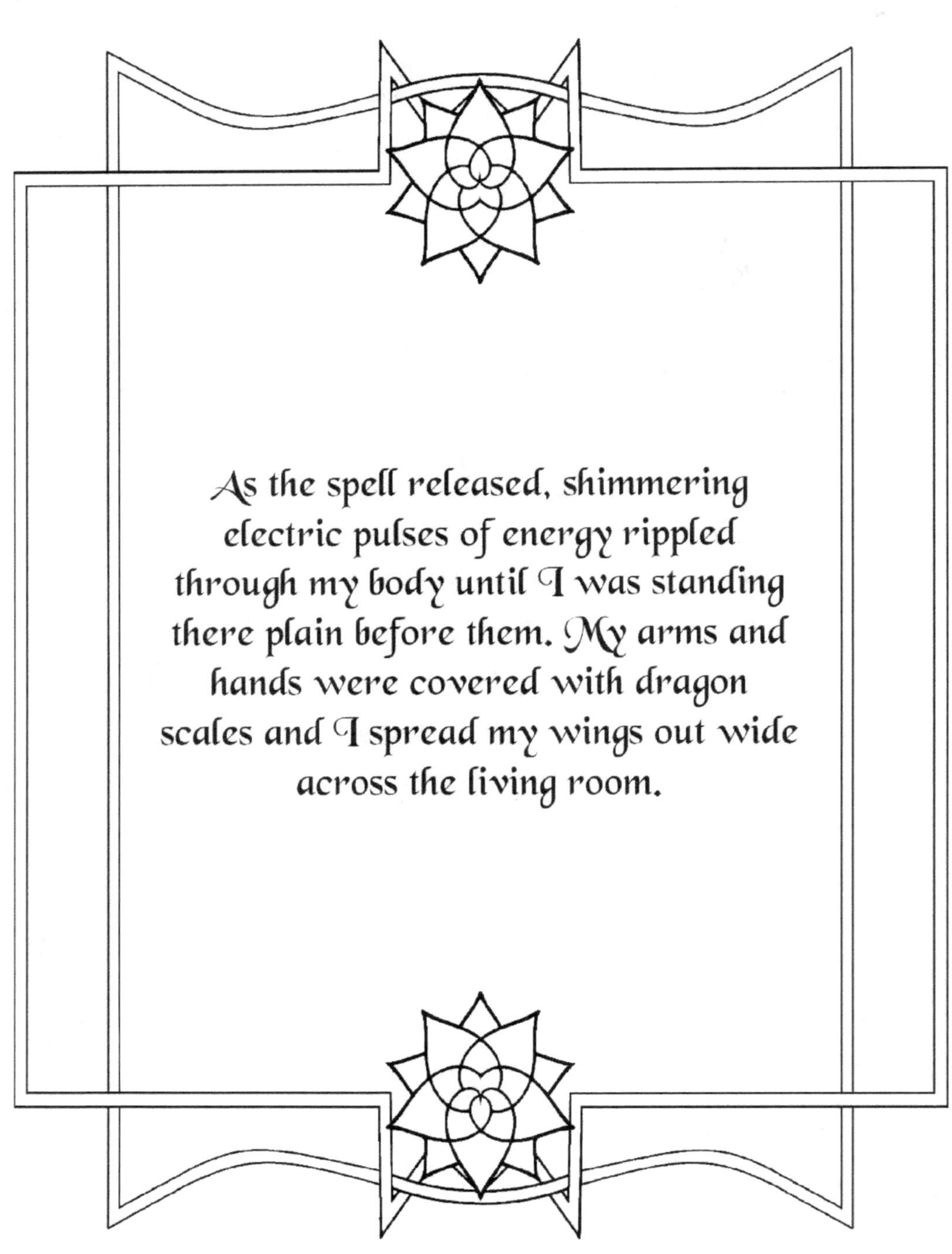

As the spell released, shimmering electric pulses of energy rippled through my body until I was standing there plain before them. My arms and hands were covered with dragon scales and I spread my wings out wide across the living room.

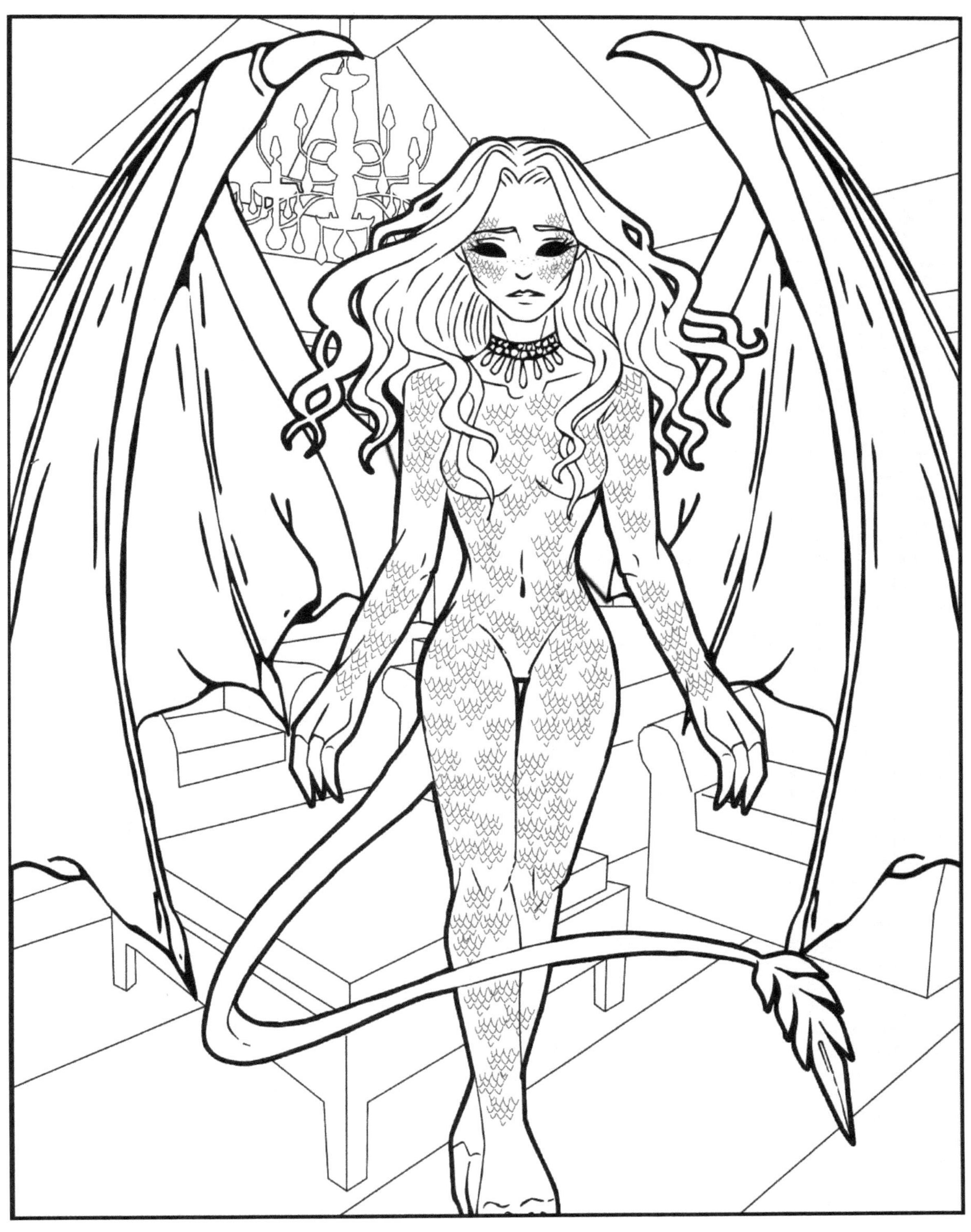

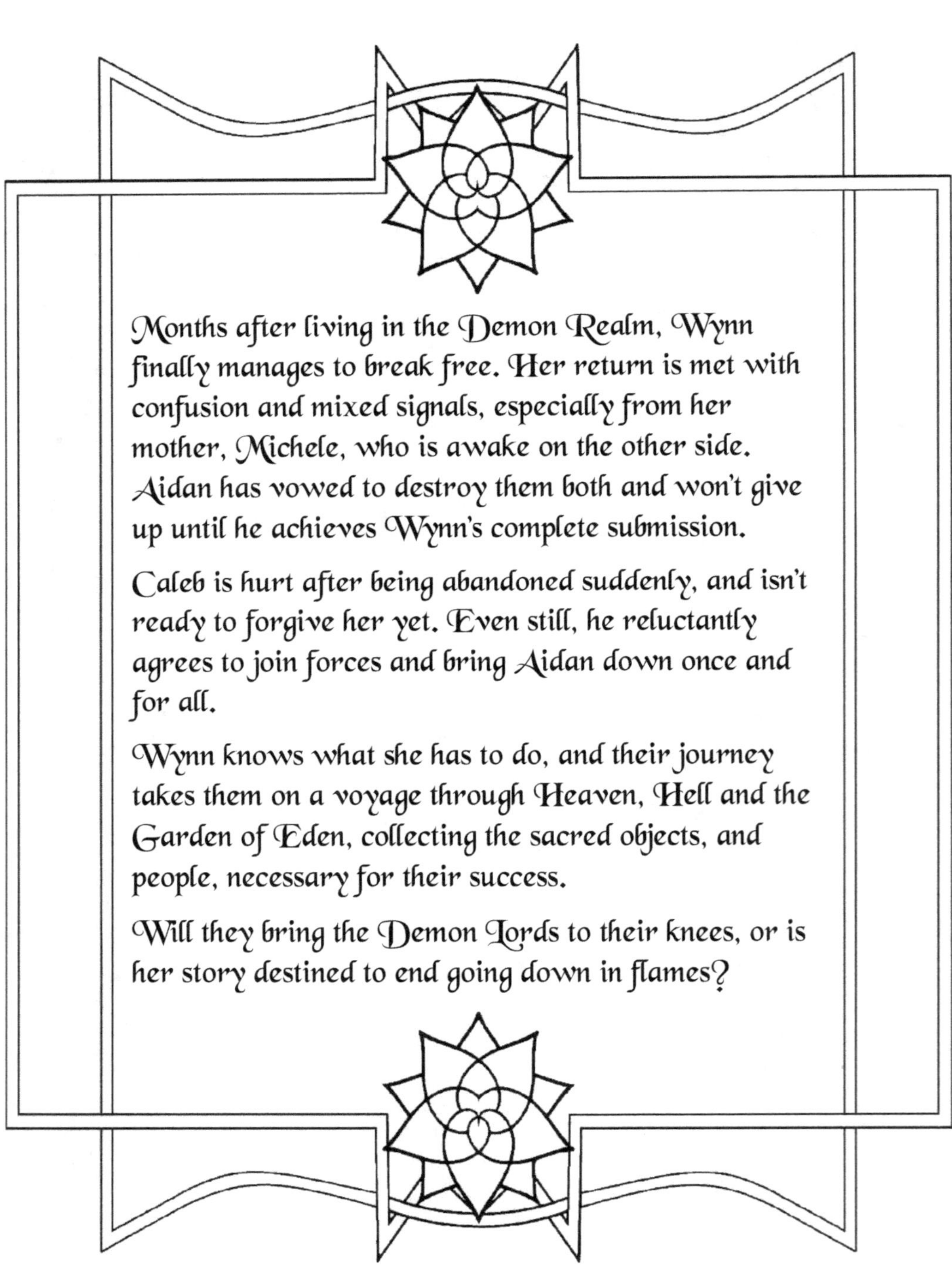

Months after living in the Demon Realm, Wynn finally manages to break free. Her return is met with confusion and mixed signals, especially from her mother, Michele, who is awake on the other side. Aidan has vowed to destroy them both and won't give up until he achieves Wynn's complete submission.

Caleb is hurt after being abandoned suddenly, and isn't ready to forgive her yet. Even still, he reluctantly agrees to join forces and bring Aidan down once and for all.

Wynn knows what she has to do, and their journey takes them on a voyage through Heaven, Hell and the Garden of Eden, collecting the sacred objects, and people, necessary for their success.

Will they bring the Demon Lords to their knees, or is her story destined to end going down in flames?

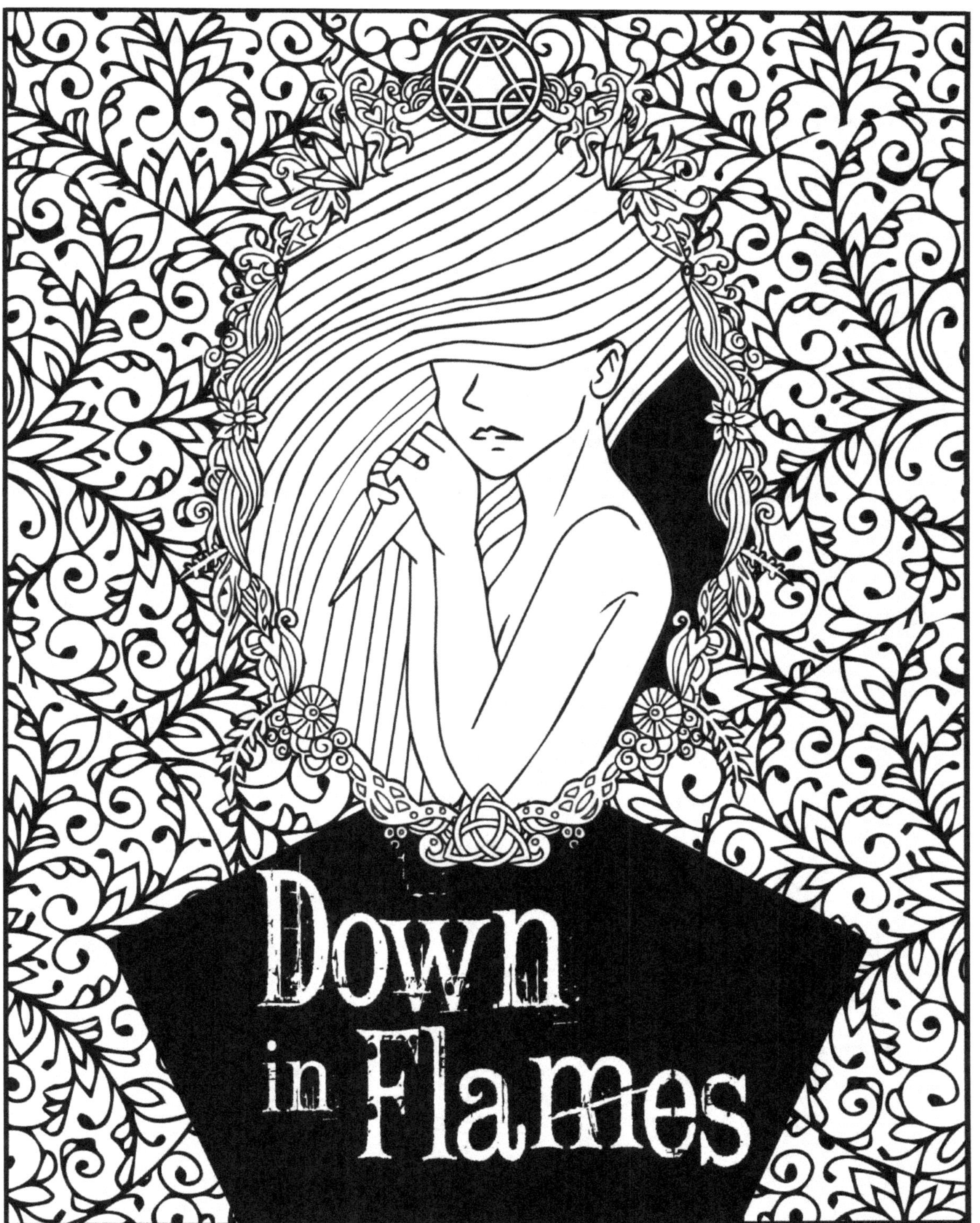
Down
in Flames

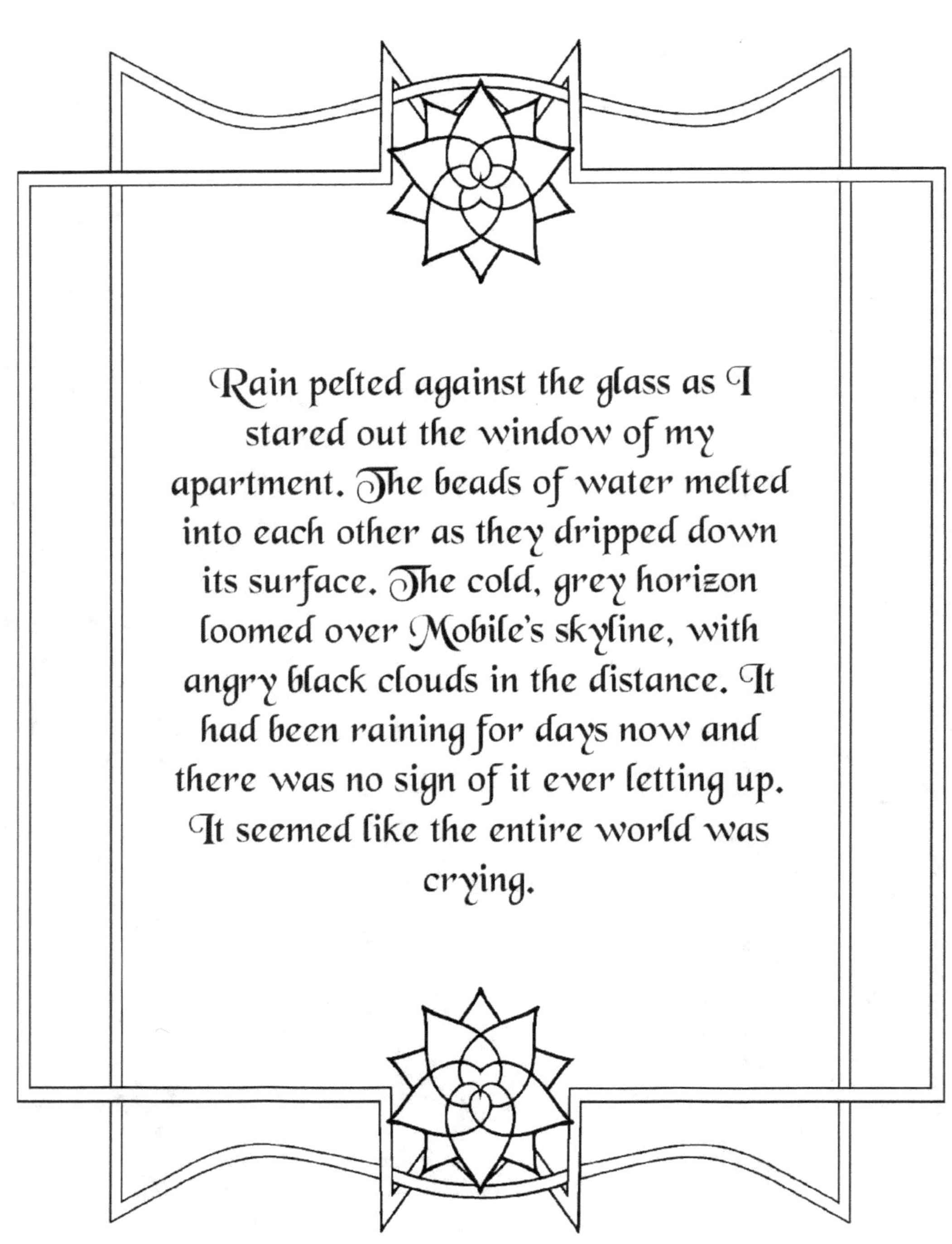

Rain pelted against the glass as I stared out the window of my apartment. The beads of water melted into each other as they dripped down its surface. The cold, grey horizon loomed over Mobile's skyline, with angry black clouds in the distance. It had been raining for days now and there was no sign of it ever letting up. It seemed like the entire world was crying.

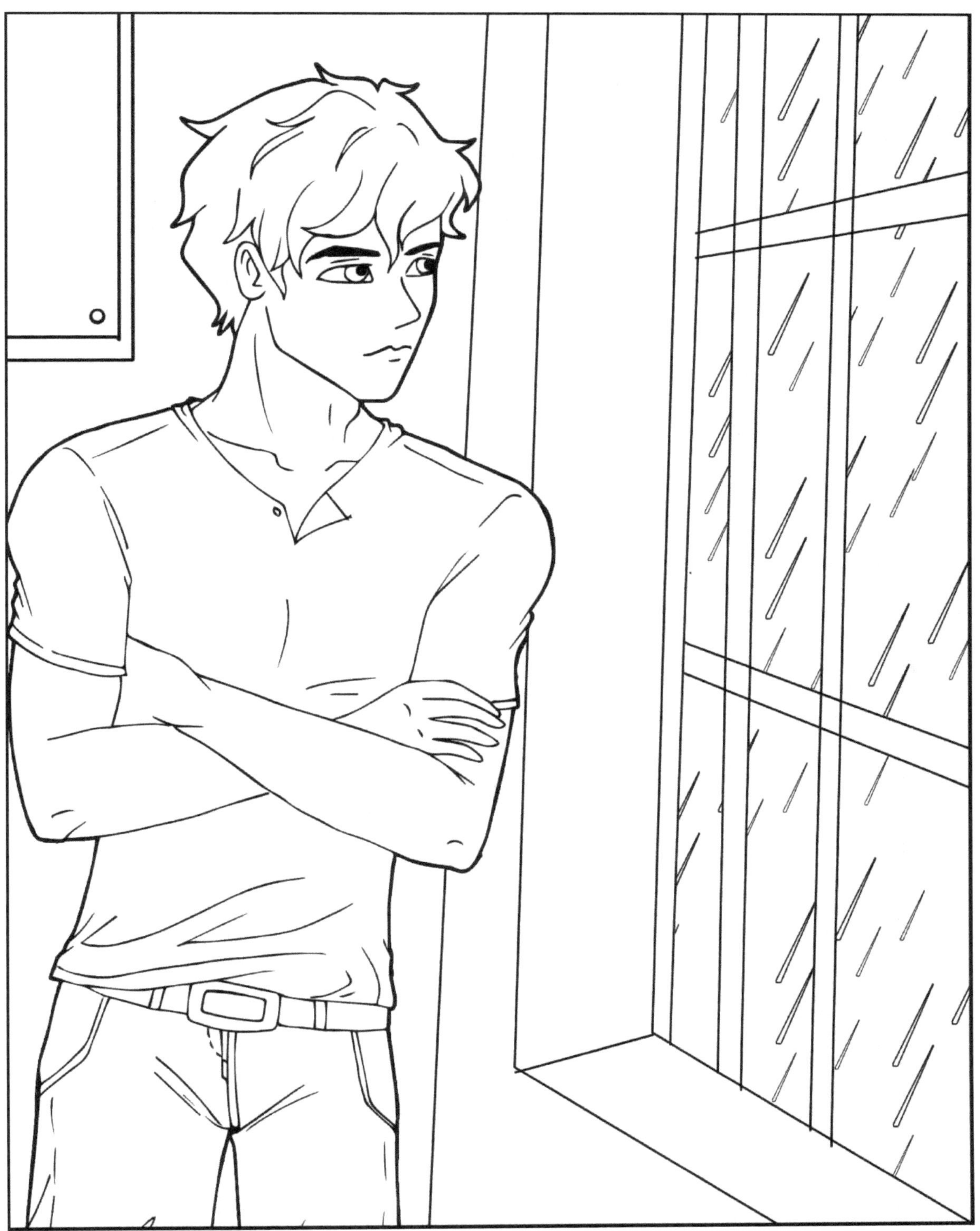

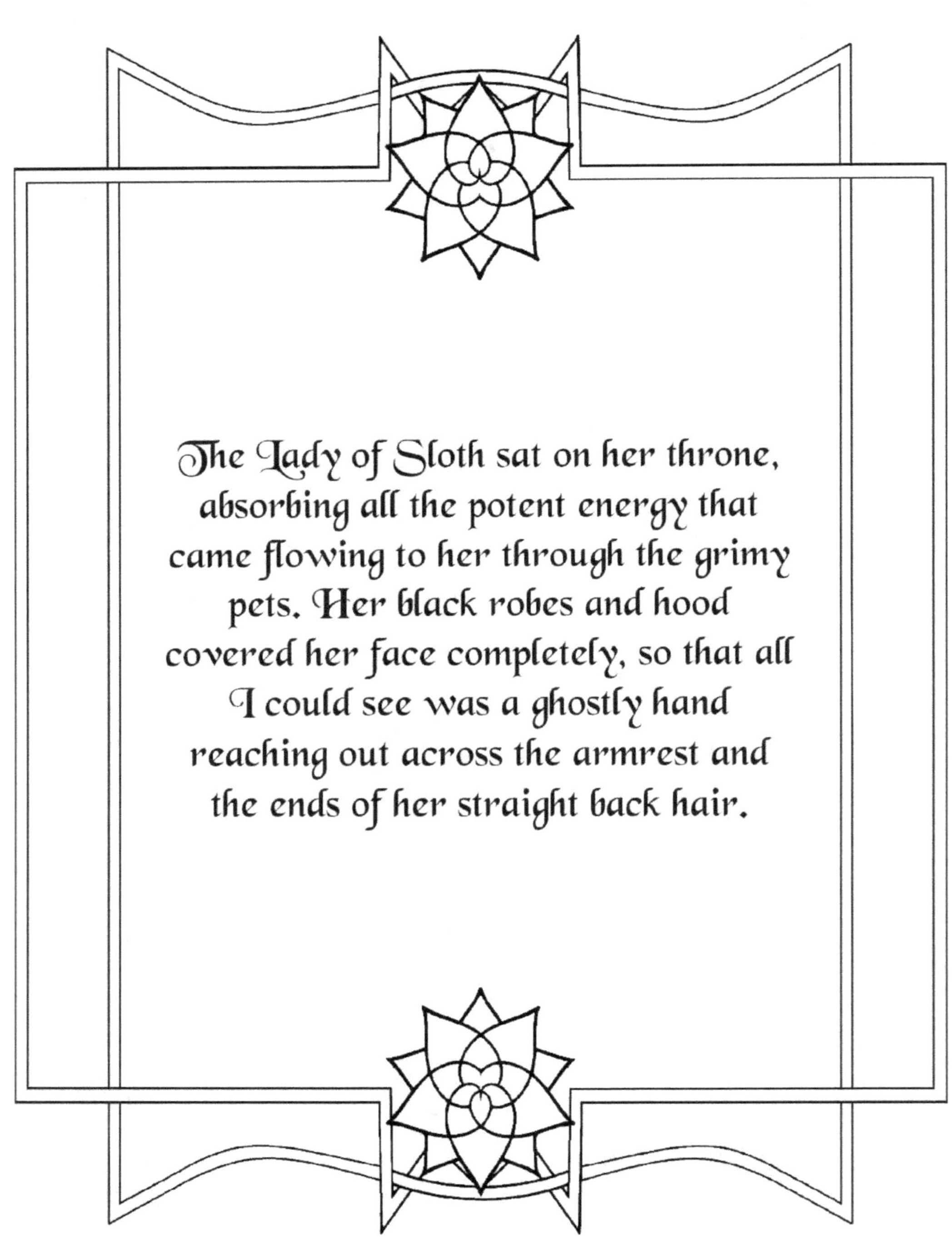

The Lady of Sloth sat on her throne, absorbing all the potent energy that came flowing to her through the grimy pets. Her black robes and hood covered her face completely, so that all I could see was a ghostly hand reaching out across the armrest and the ends of her straight back hair.

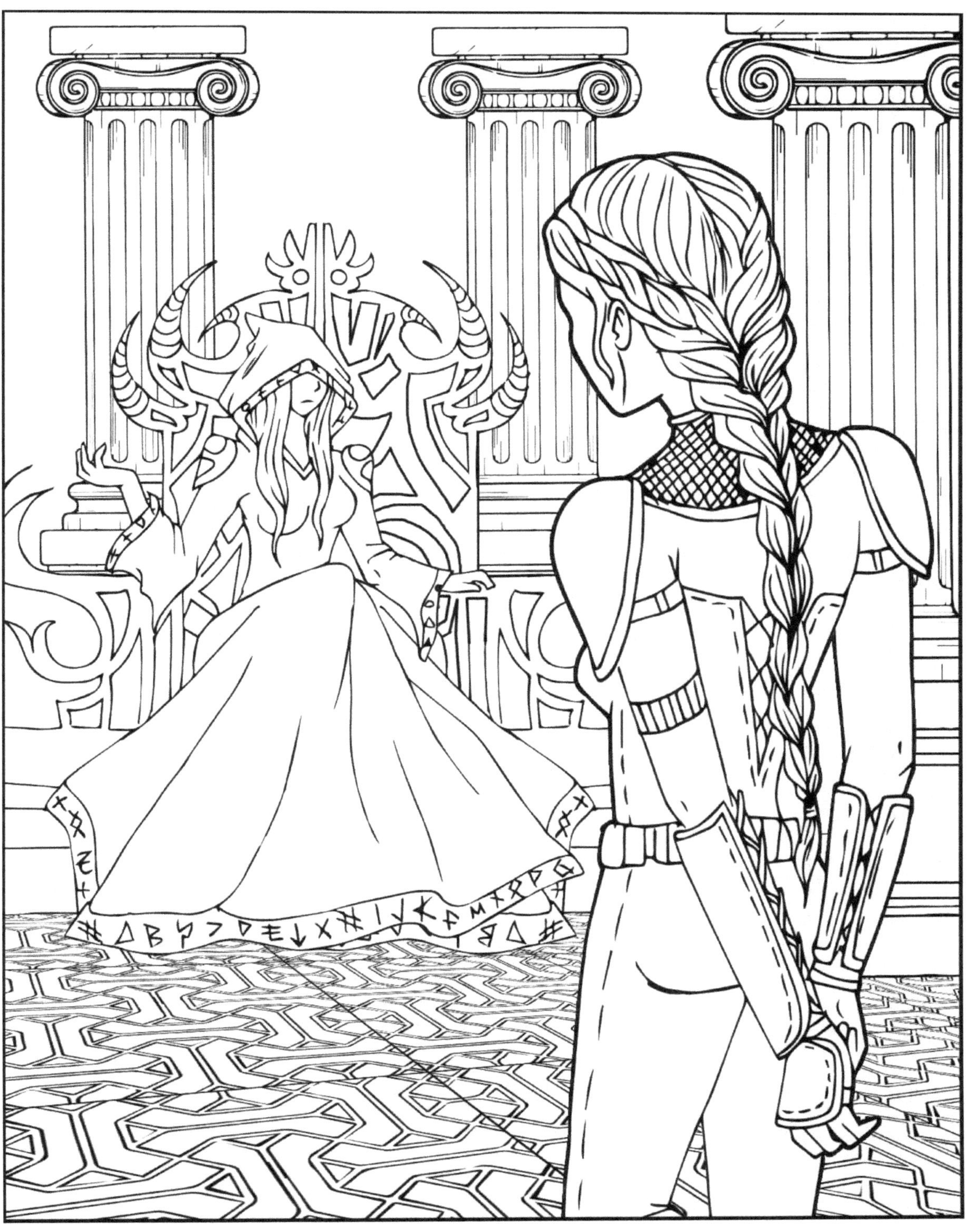

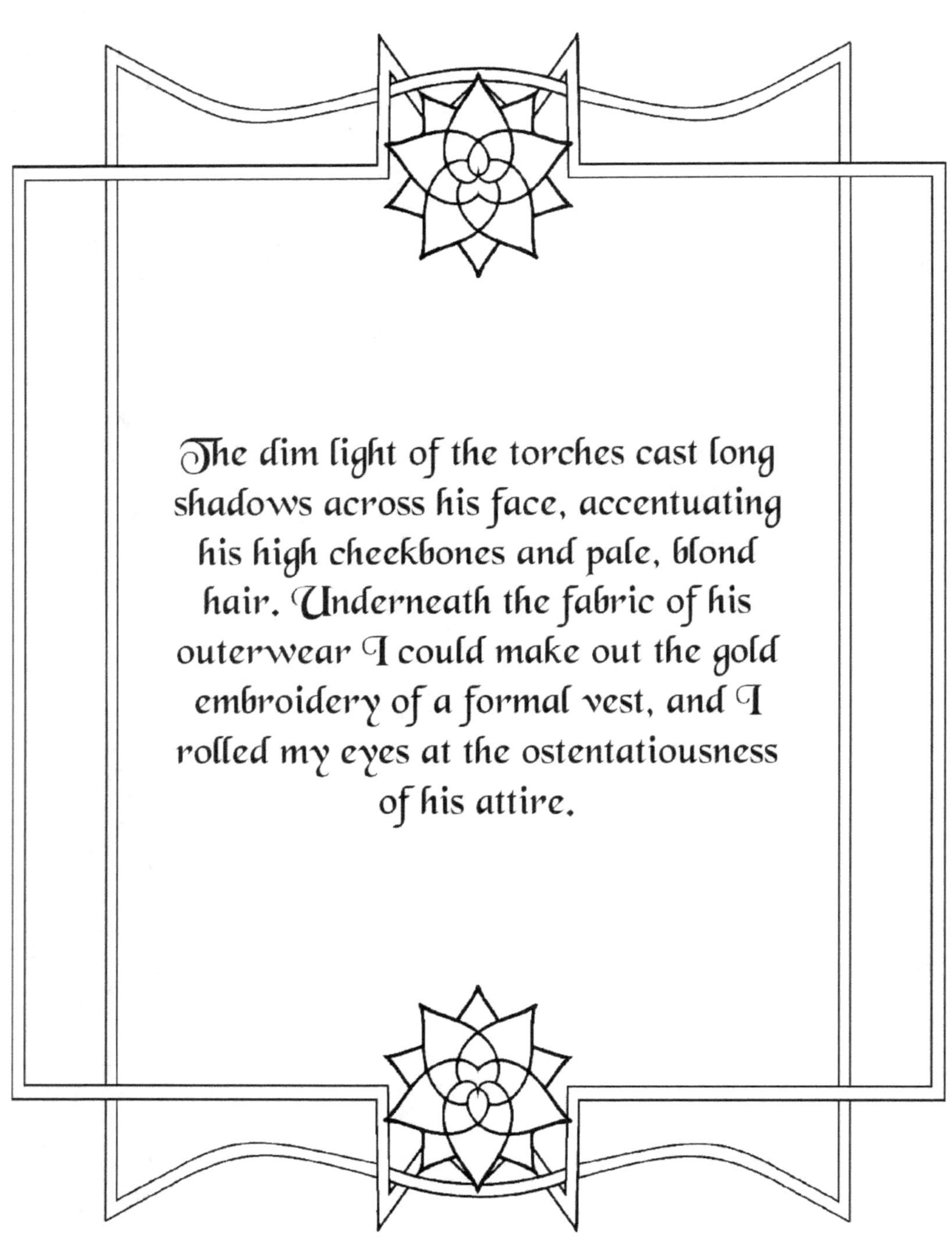

The dim light of the torches cast long shadows across his face, accentuating his high cheekbones and pale, blond hair. Underneath the fabric of his outerwear I could make out the gold embroidery of a formal vest, and I rolled my eyes at the ostentatiousness of his attire.

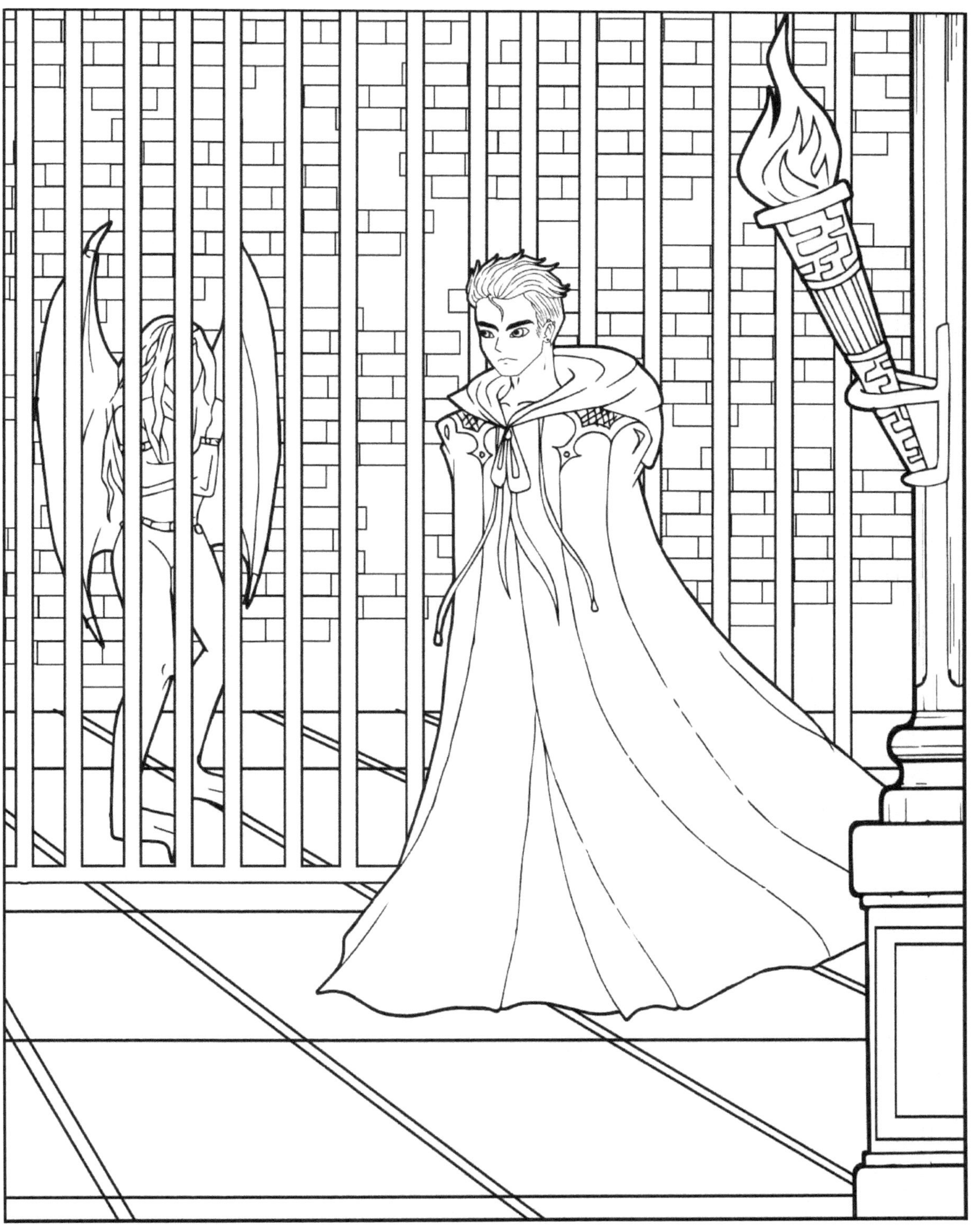

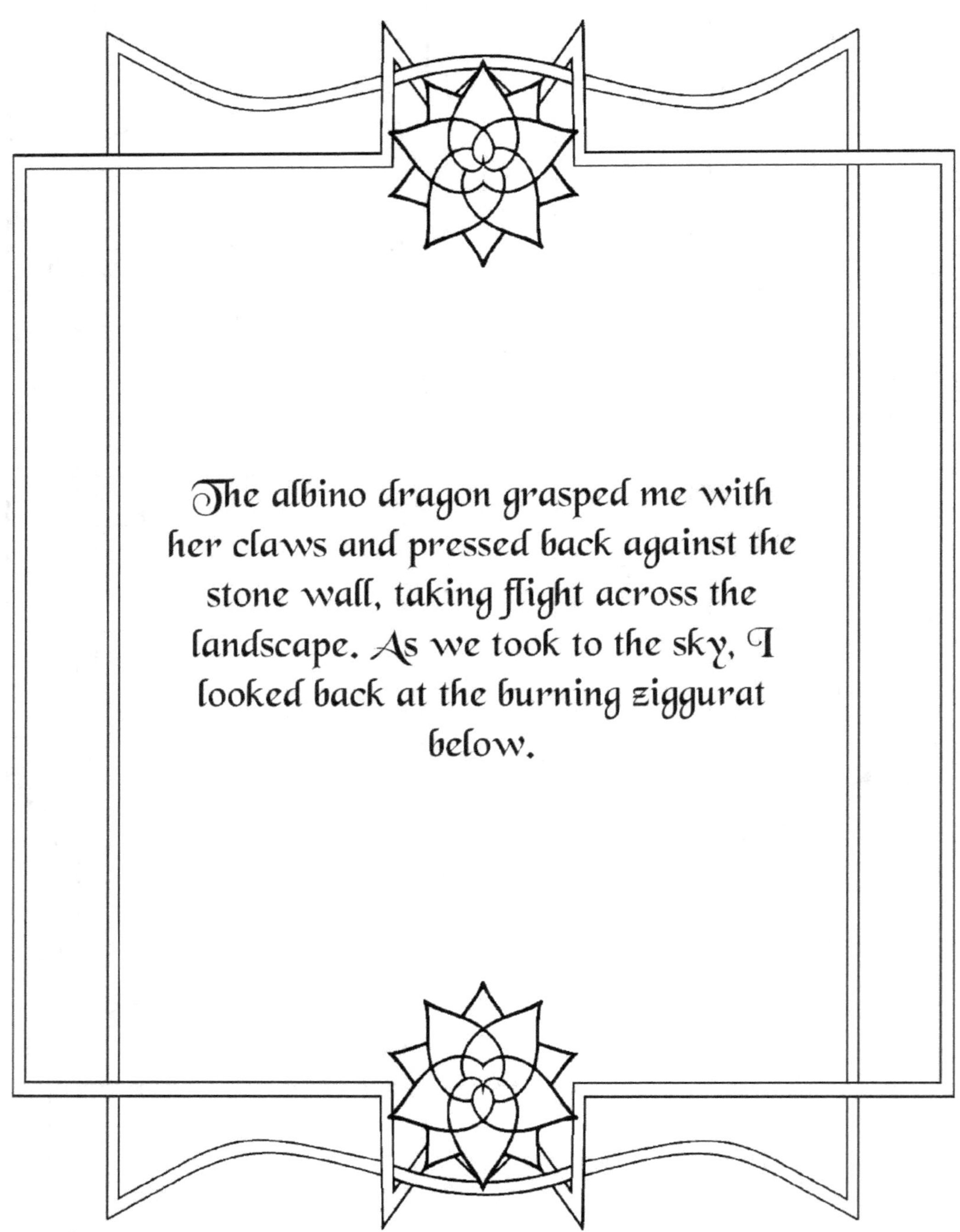

The albino dragon grasped me with her claws and pressed back against the stone wall, taking flight across the landscape. As we took to the sky, I looked back at the burning ziggurat below.

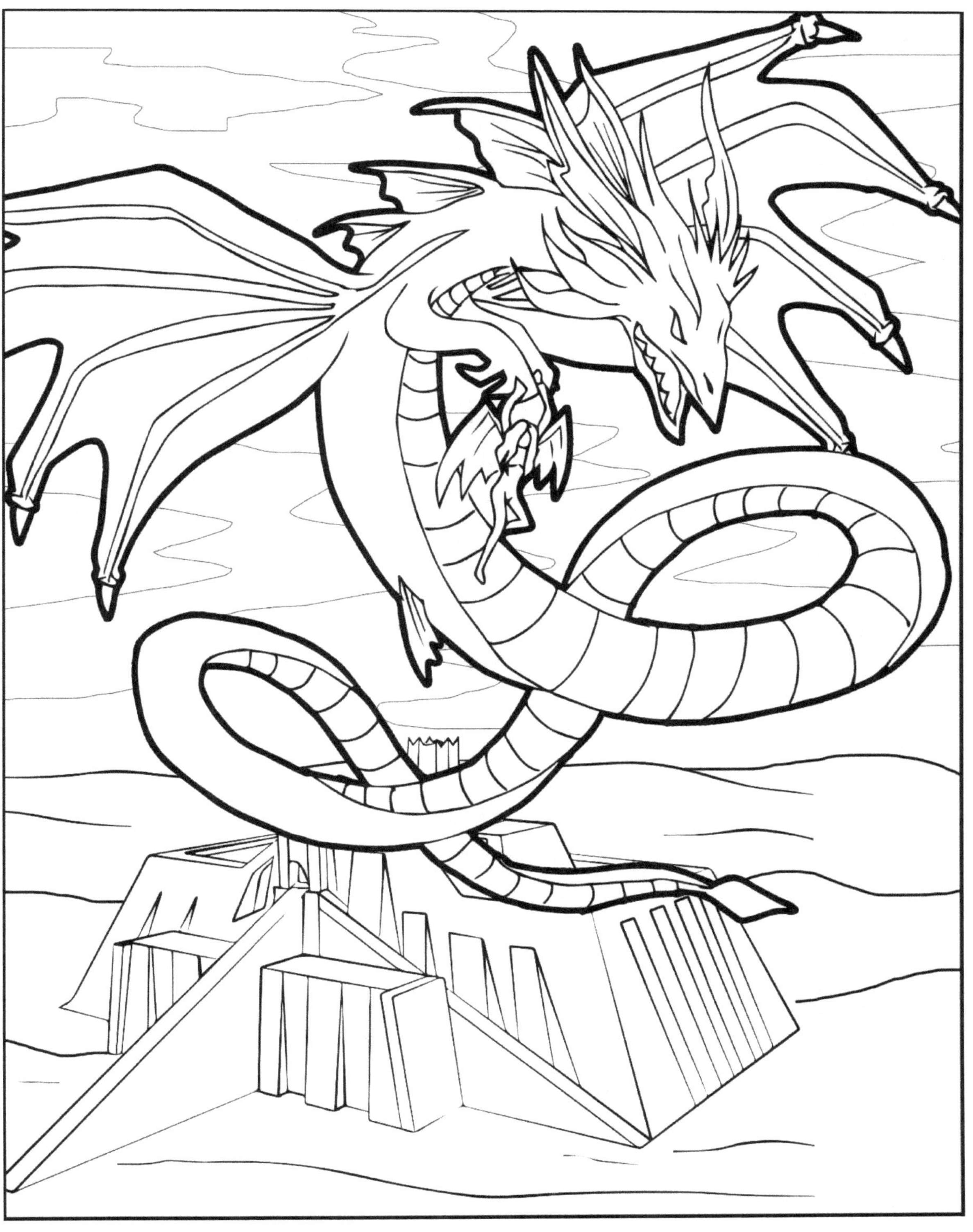

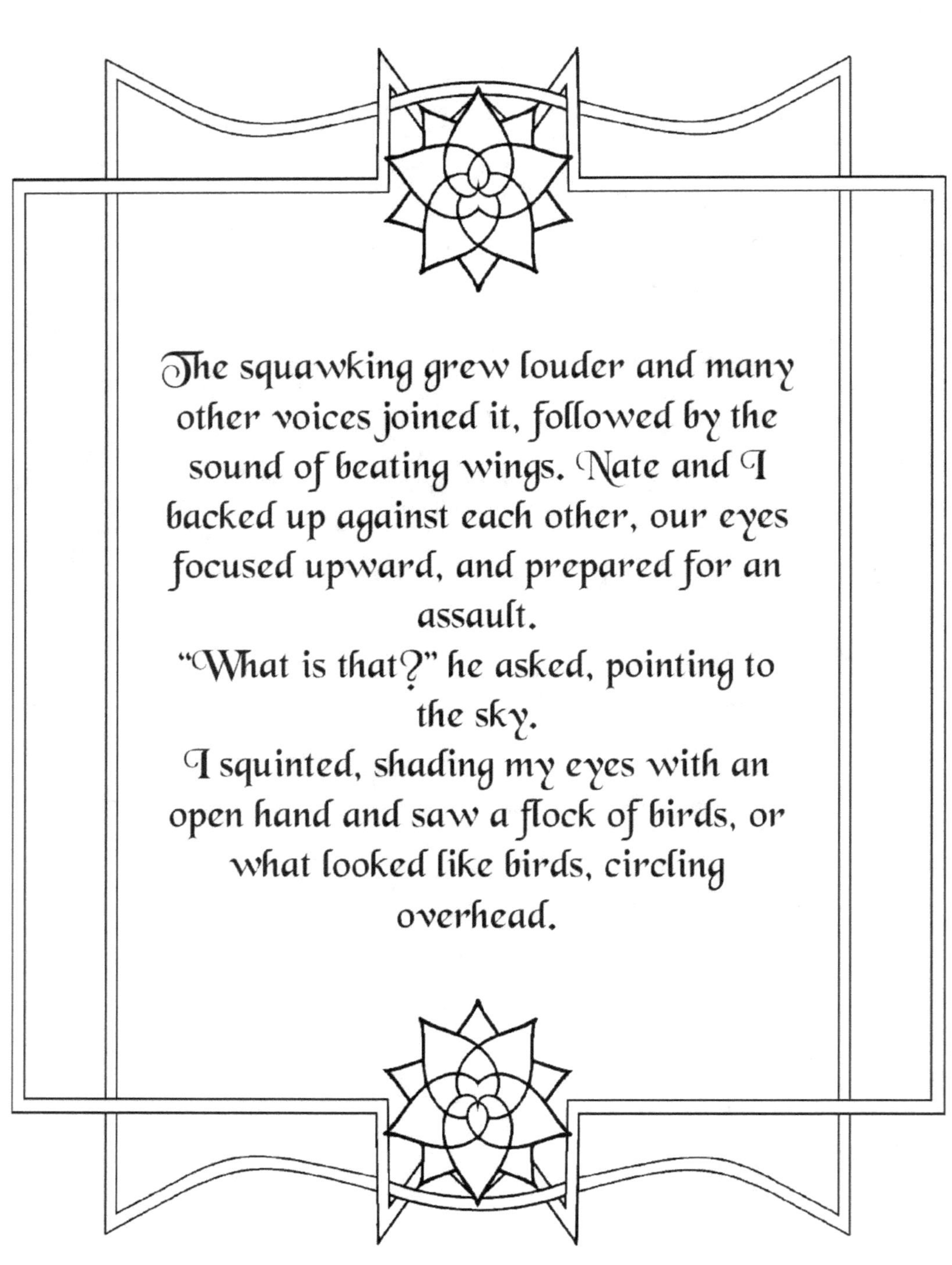

The squawking grew louder and many other voices joined it, followed by the sound of beating wings. Nate and I backed up against each other, our eyes focused upward, and prepared for an assault.

"What is that?" he asked, pointing to the sky.

I squinted, shading my eyes with an open hand and saw a flock of birds, or what looked like birds, circling overhead.

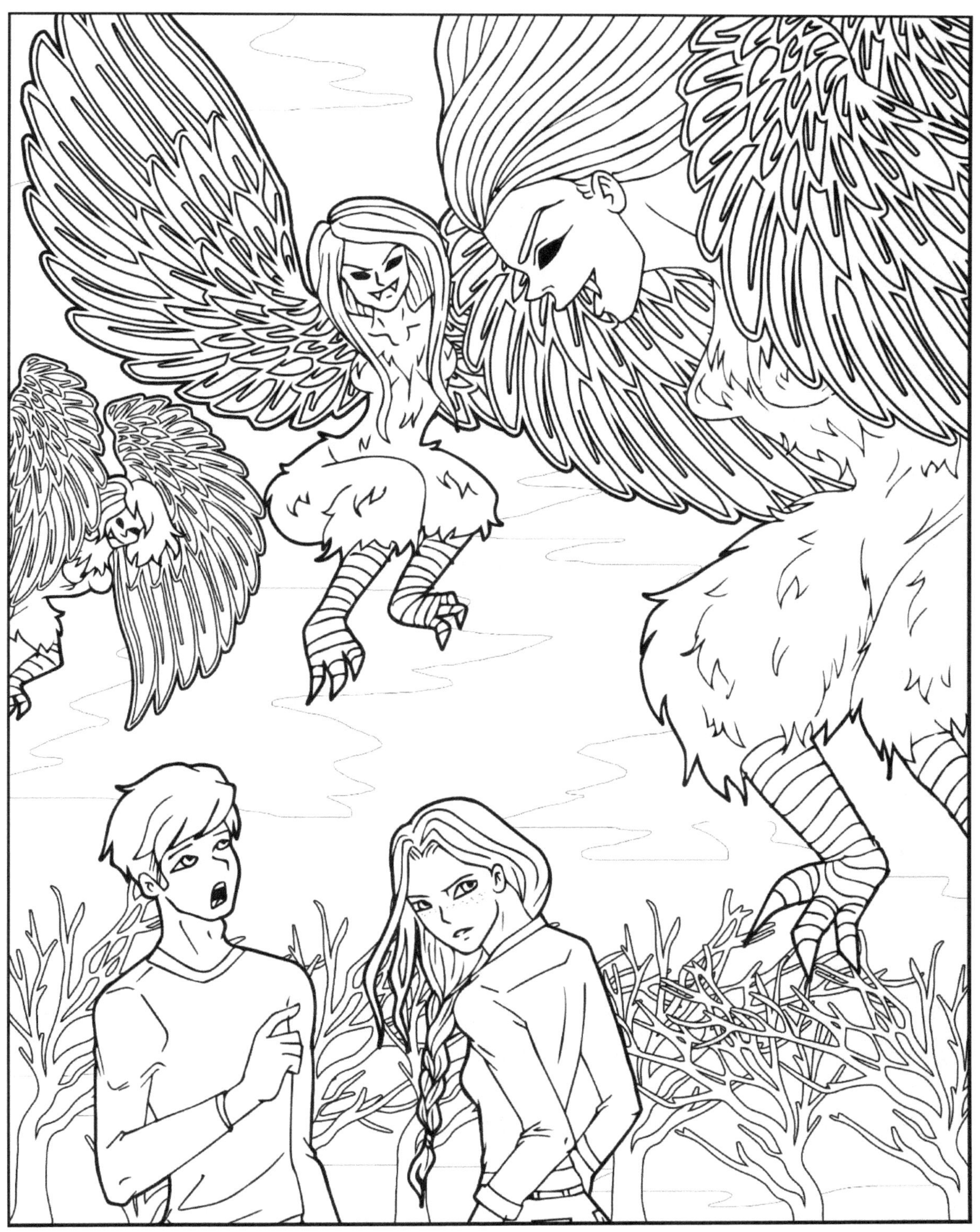

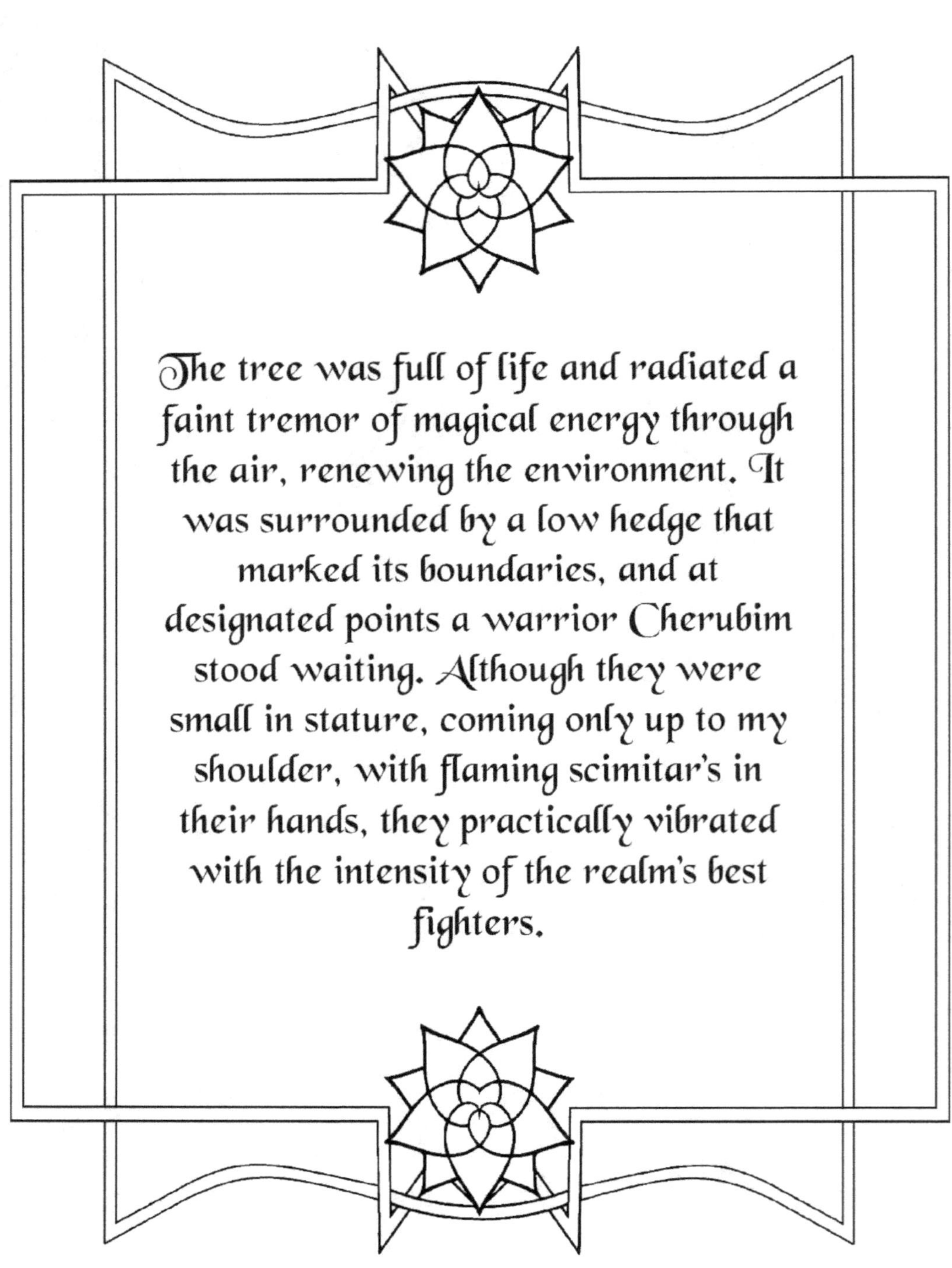

The tree was full of life and radiated a faint tremor of magical energy through the air, renewing the environment. It was surrounded by a low hedge that marked its boundaries, and at designated points a warrior Cherubim stood waiting. Although they were small in stature, coming only up to my shoulder, with flaming scimitar's in their hands, they practically vibrated with the intensity of the realm's best fighters.

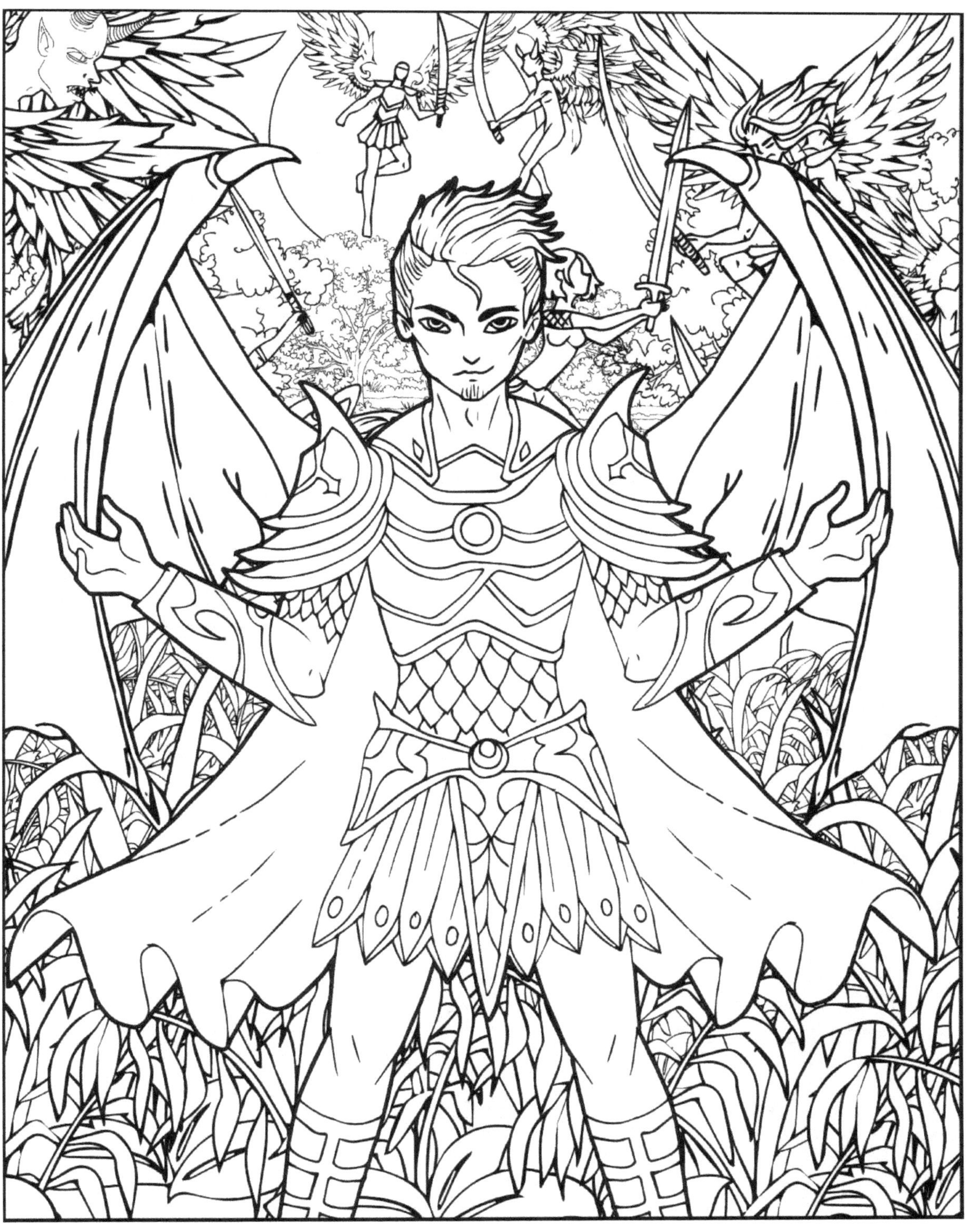

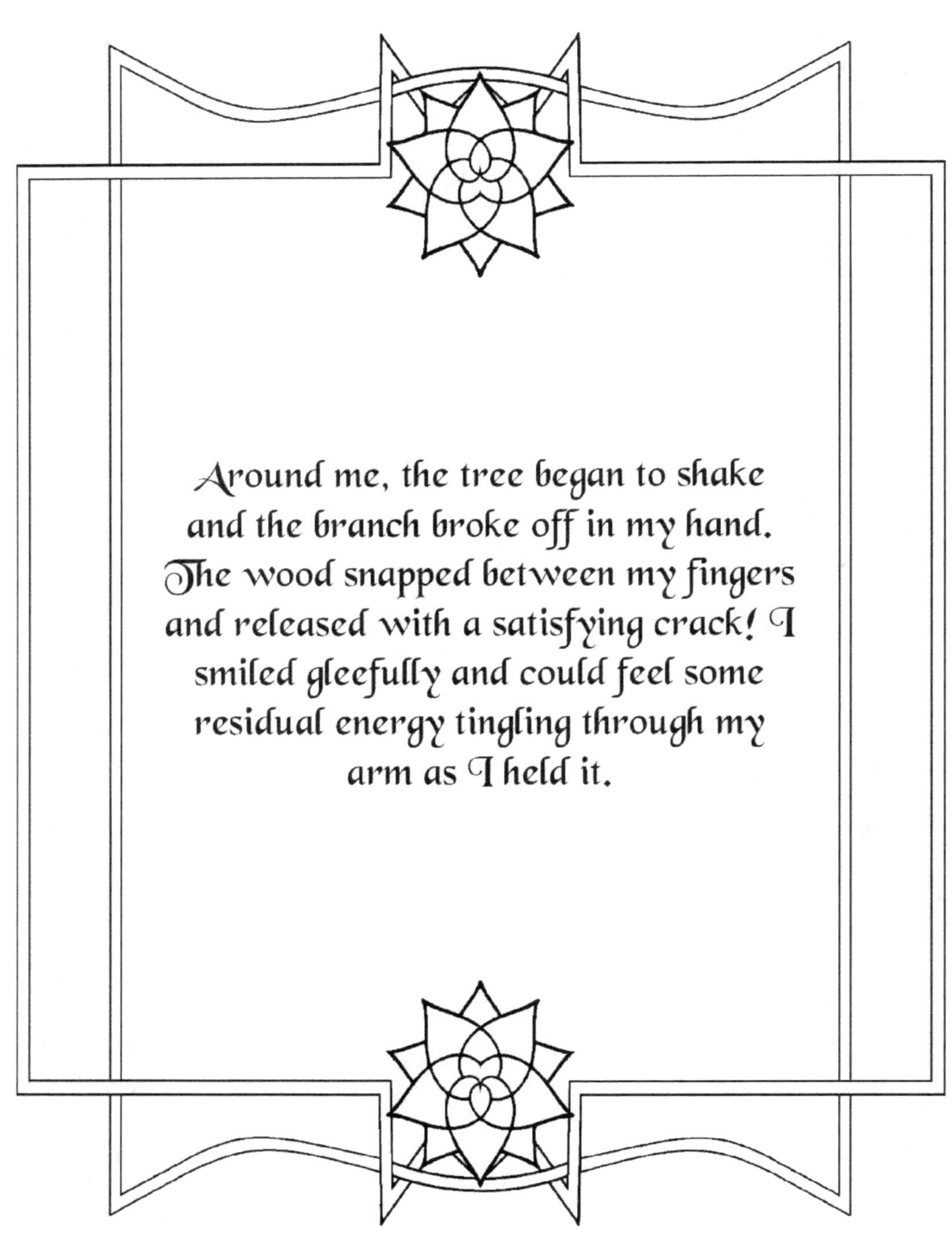

Around me, the tree began to shake and the branch broke off in my hand. The wood snapped between my fingers and released with a satisfying crack! I smiled gleefully and could feel some residual energy tingling through my arm as I held it.

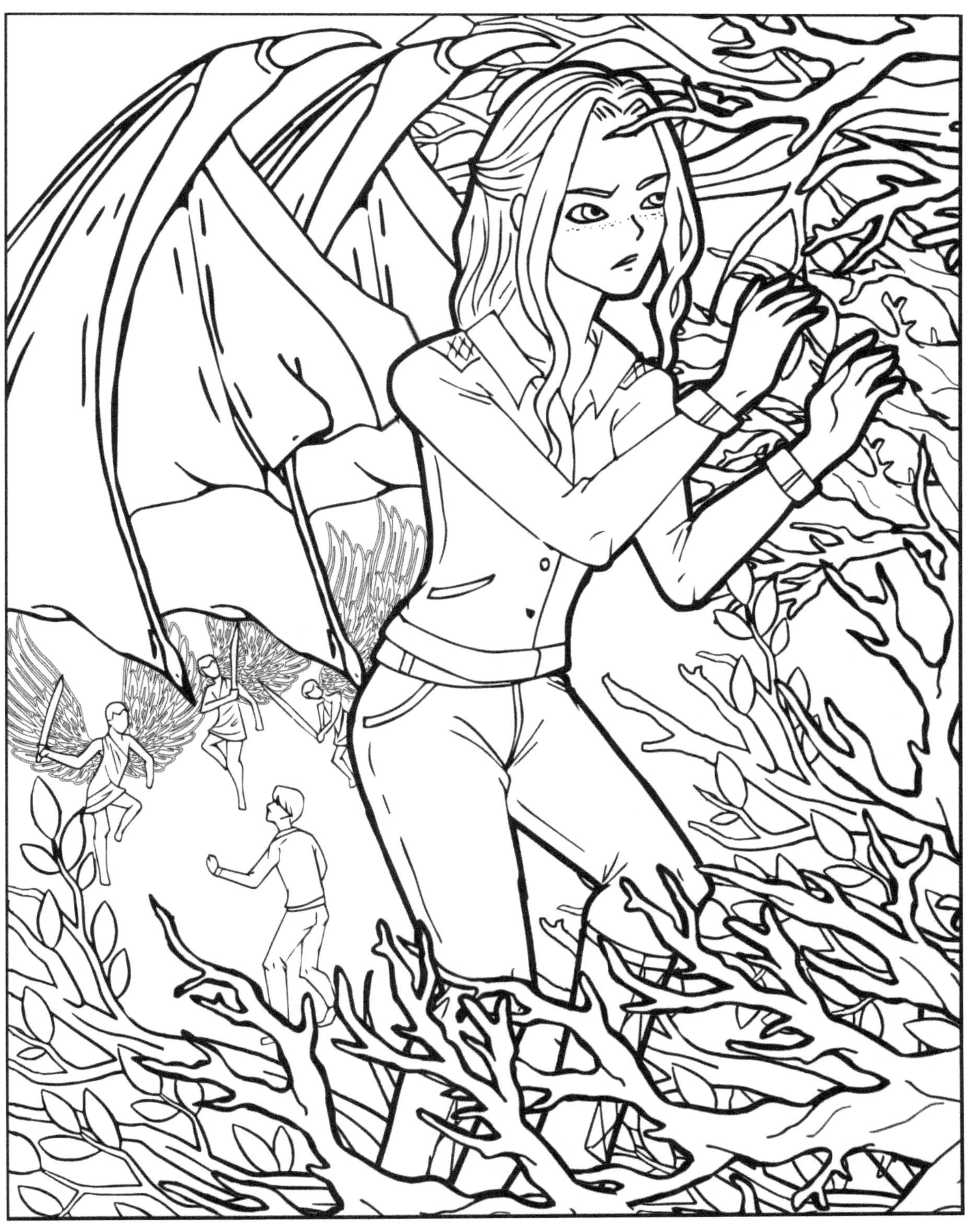

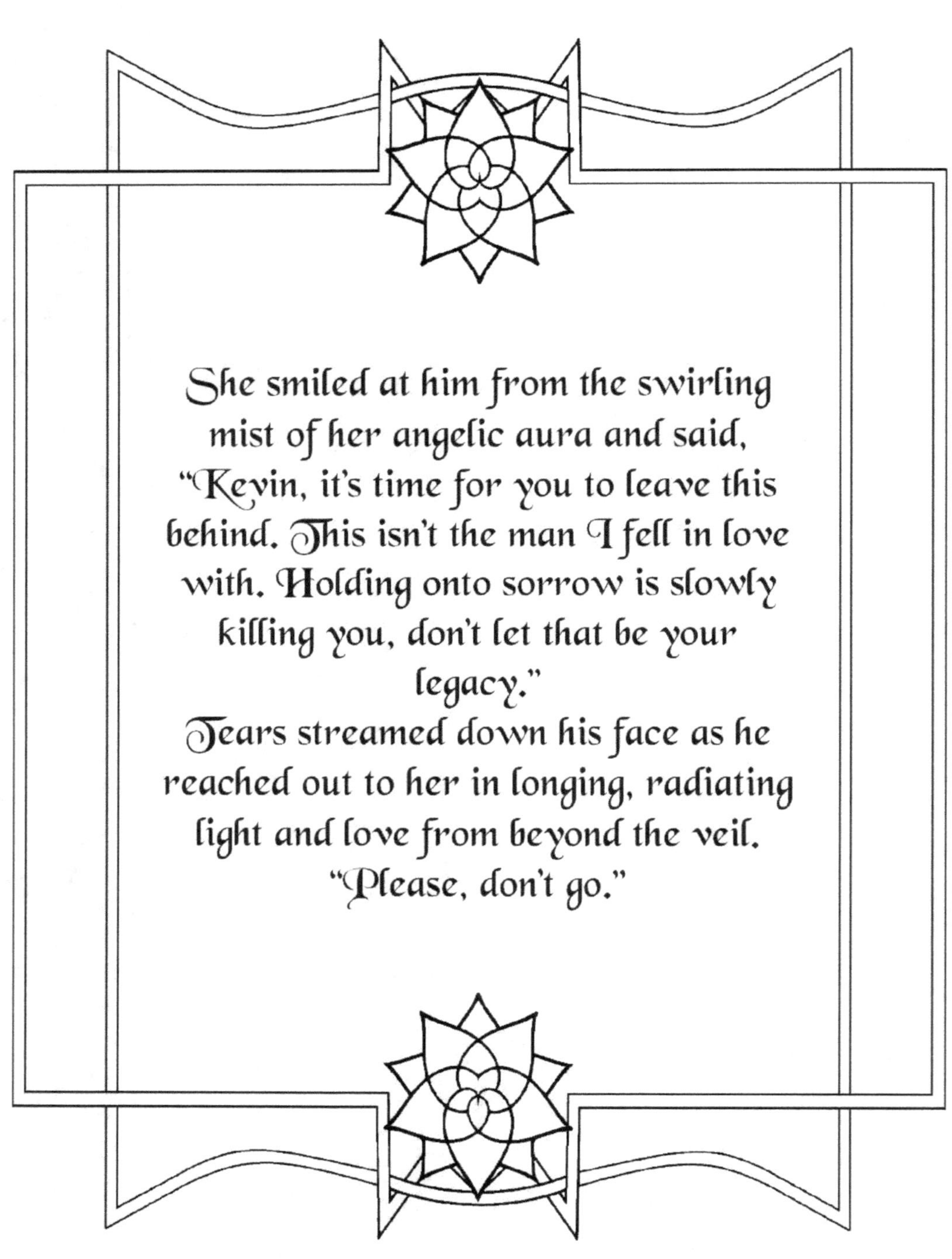

She smiled at him from the swirling mist of her angelic aura and said, "Kevin, it's time for you to leave this behind. This isn't the man I fell in love with. Holding onto sorrow is slowly killing you, don't let that be your legacy."

Tears streamed down his face as he reached out to her in longing, radiating light and love from beyond the veil.

"Please, don't go."

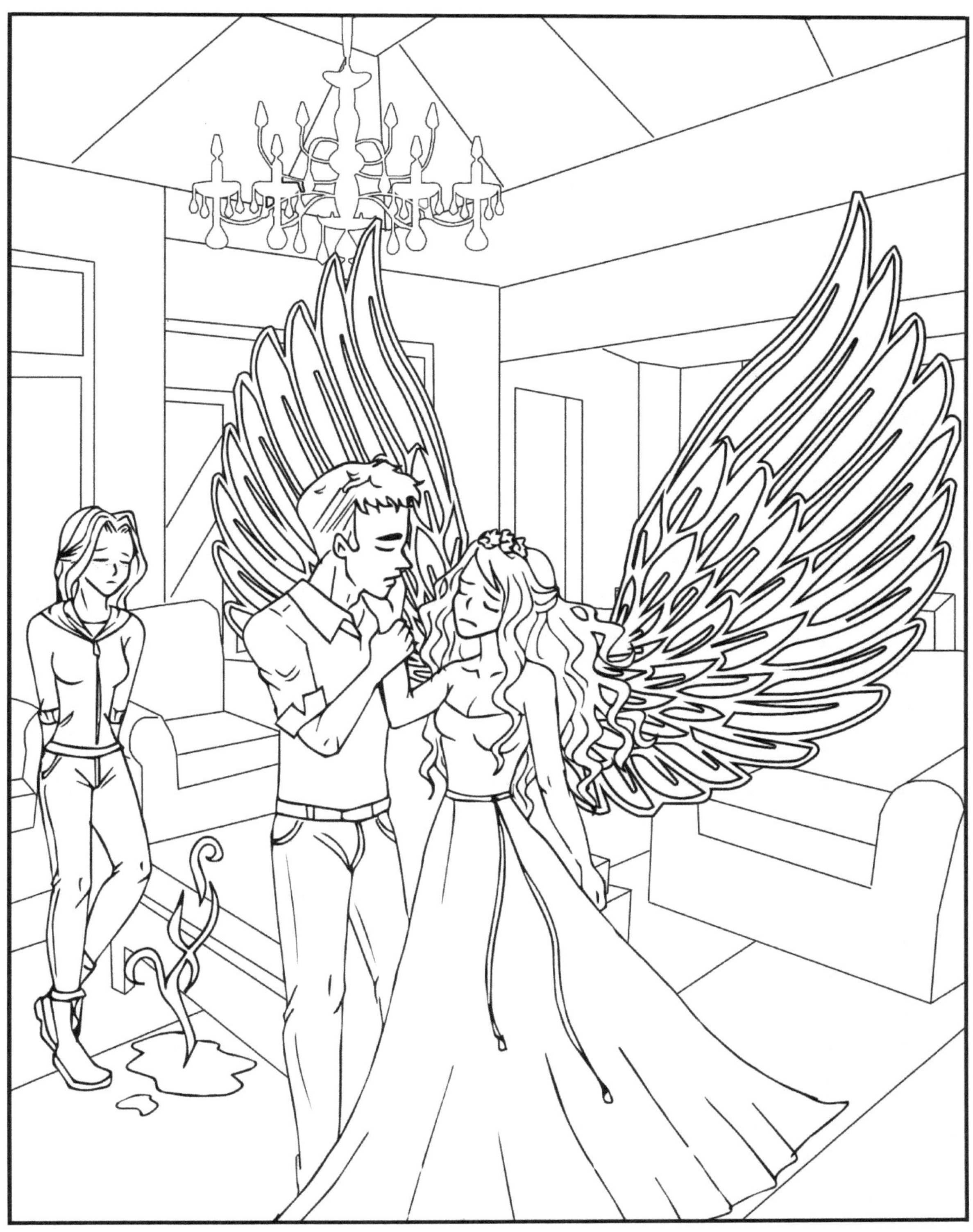

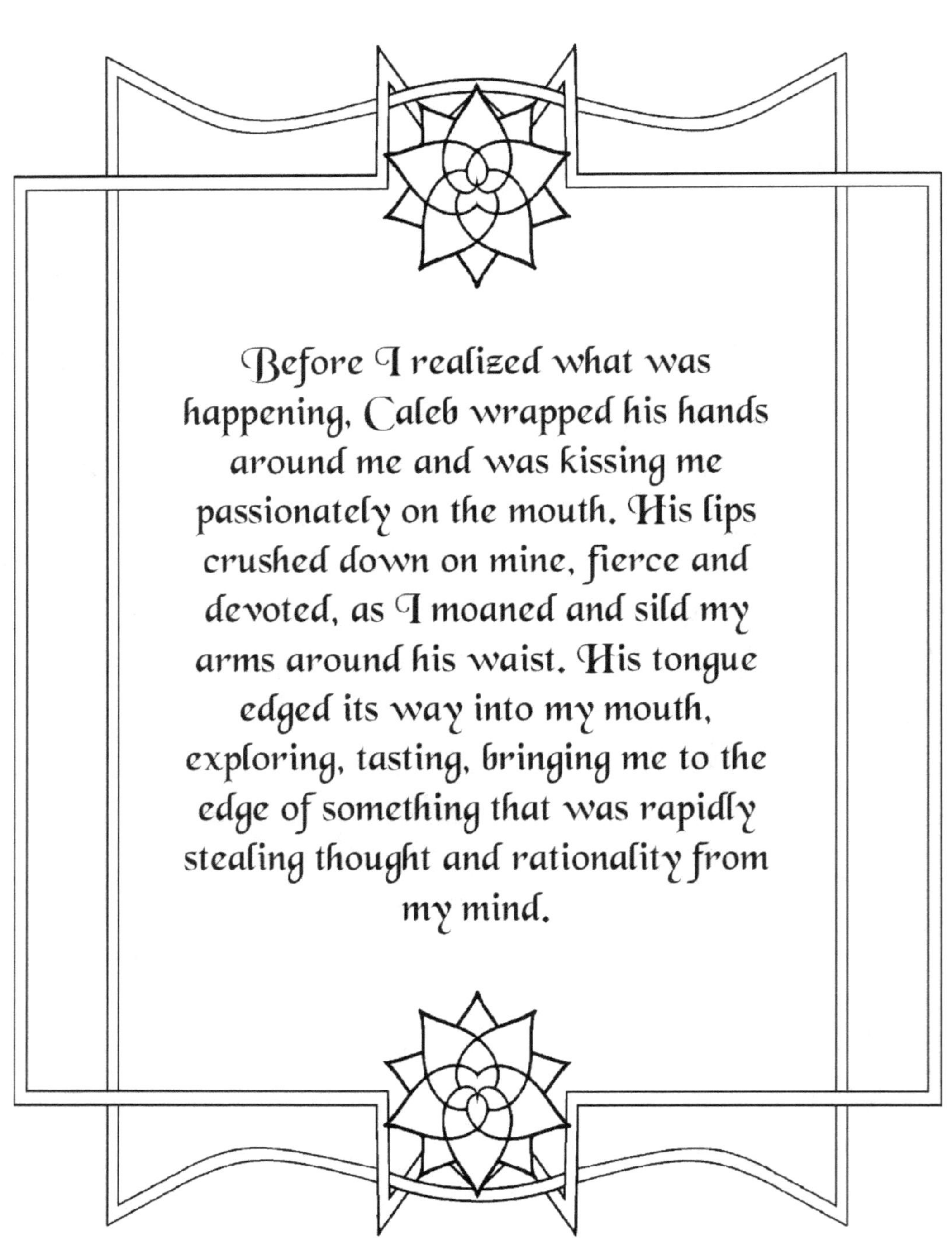

Before I realized what was happening, Caleb wrapped his hands around me and was kissing me passionately on the mouth. His lips crushed down on mine, fierce and devoted, as I moaned and sild my arms around his waist. His tongue edged its way into my mouth, exploring, tasting, bringing me to the edge of something that was rapidly stealing thought and rationality from my mind.

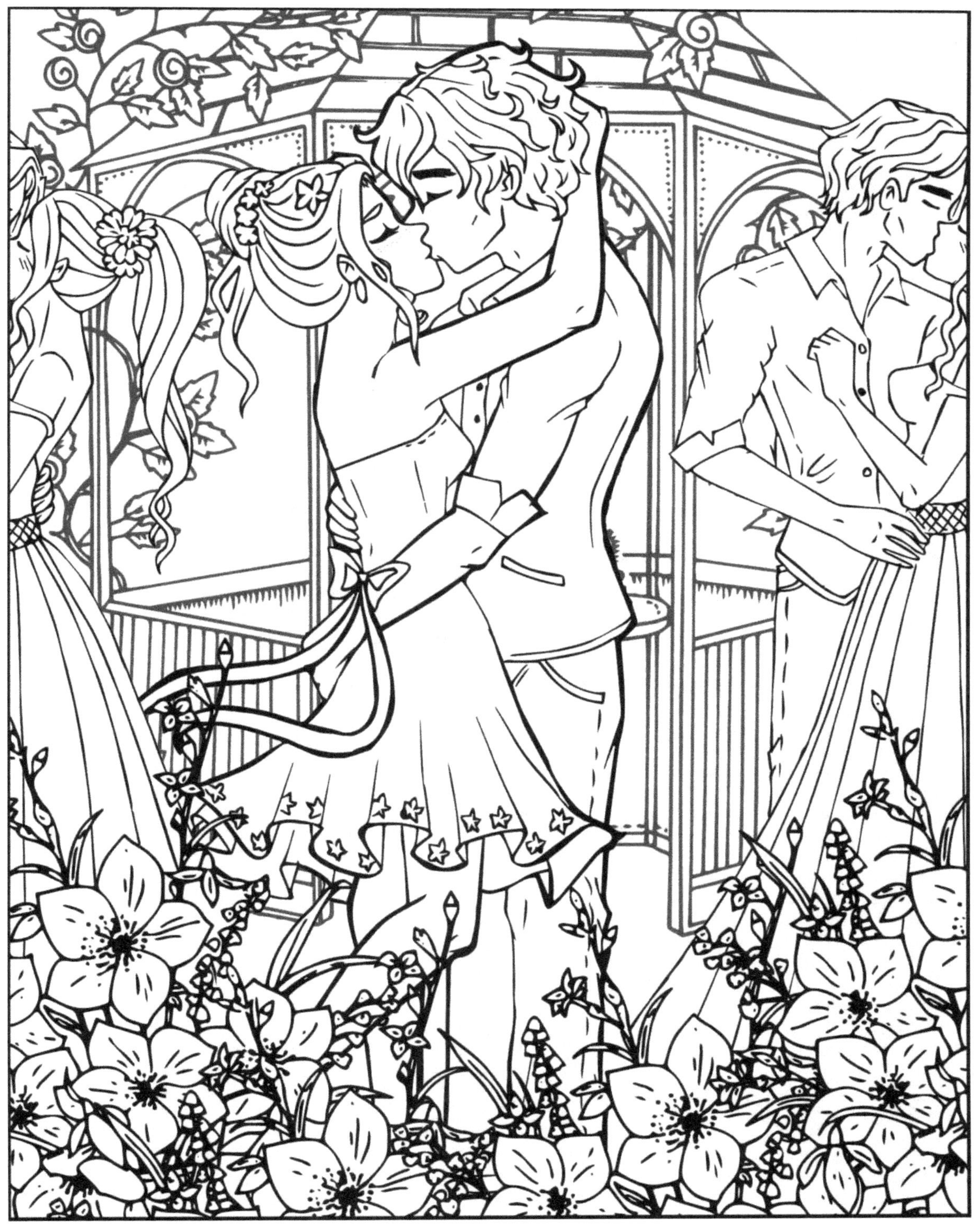

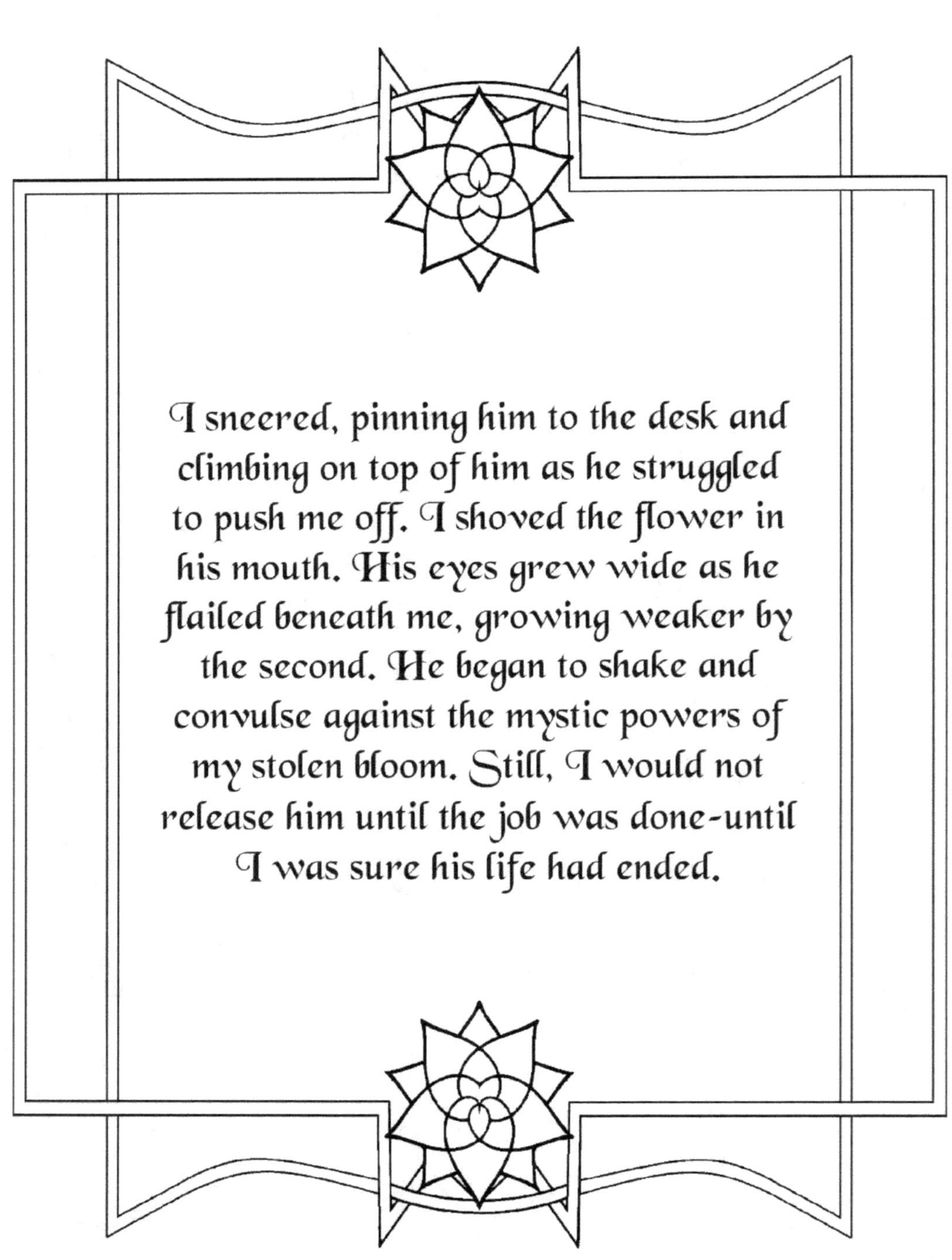

I sneered, pinning him to the desk and climbing on top of him as he struggled to push me off. I shoved the flower in his mouth. His eyes grew wide as he flailed beneath me, growing weaker by the second. He began to shake and convulse against the mystic powers of my stolen bloom. Still, I would not release him until the job was done-until I was sure his life had ended.

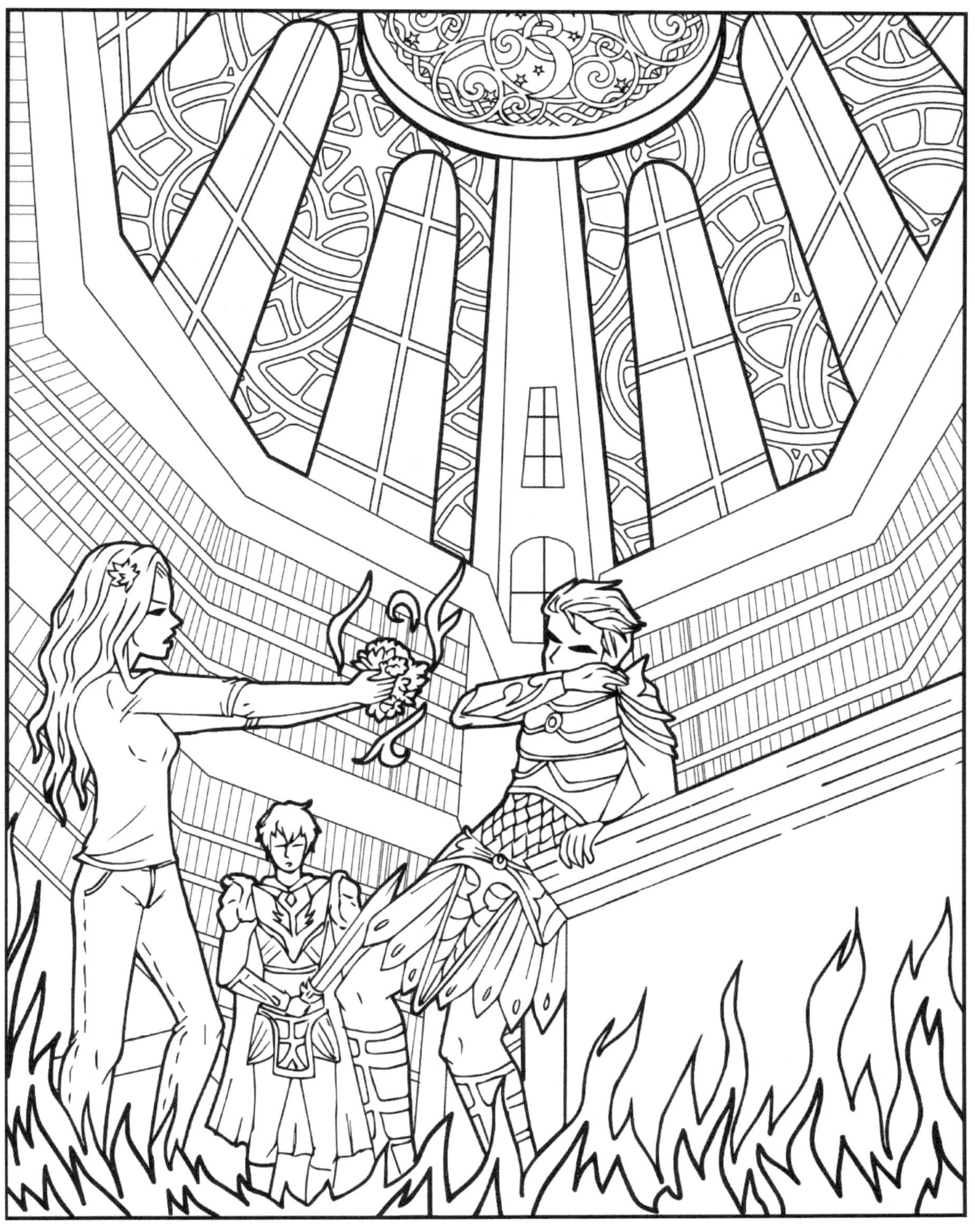

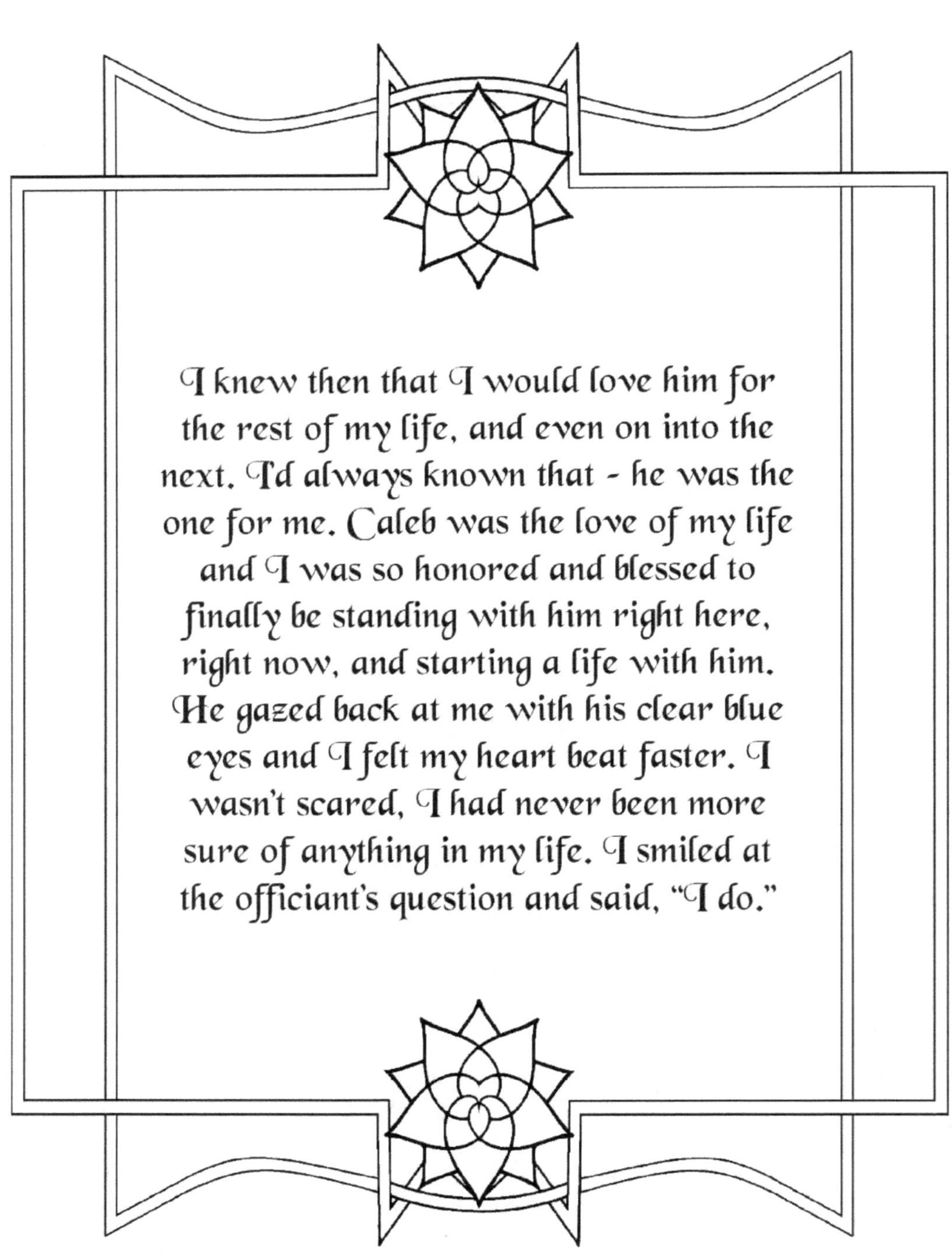

I knew then that I would love him for the rest of my life, and even on into the next. I'd always known that - he was the one for me. Caleb was the love of my life and I was so honored and blessed to finally be standing with him right here, right now, and starting a life with him. He gazed back at me with his clear blue eyes and I felt my heart beat faster. I wasn't scared, I had never been more sure of anything in my life. I smiled at the officiant's question and said, "I do."

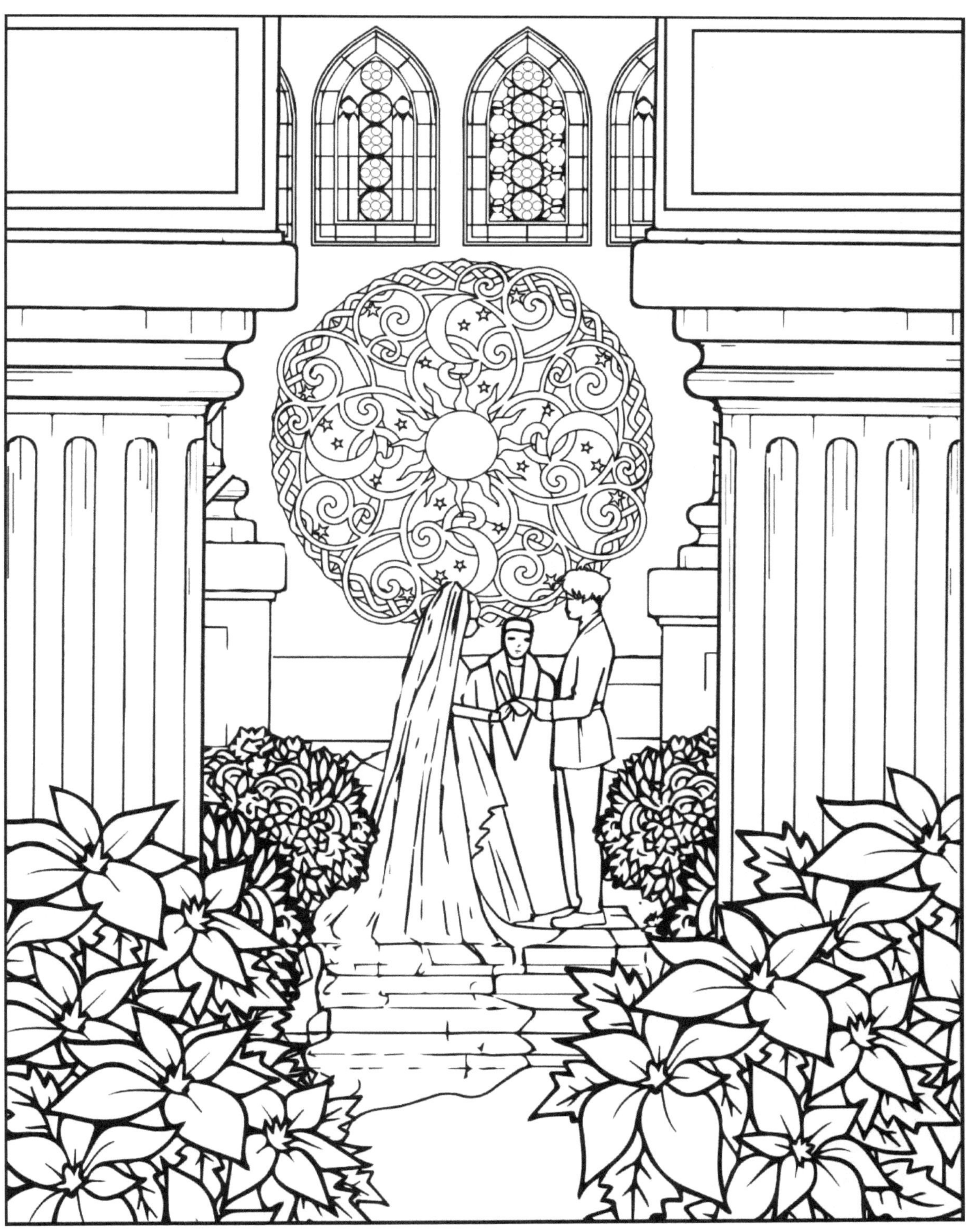

www.ingramcontent.com/pod-product-compliance
Lightning Source LLC
LaVergne TN
LVHW080316110826
845155LV00023B/131

* 9 7 8 1 9 4 2 6 2 3 9 8 4 *